...hould be returned to any Lanc...
...for... ...ng

historical mysteries...

WINNER OF THE MAL PEET CHILDREN'S AWARD

WINNER OF THE EAST ANGLIAN BOOK OF THE YEAR

"Fans of Emma Carroll will adore this historical tale of derring-do and righted wrongs."
The Times

"Enchanting adventure...cleverly created, full of secrets, mystery and memorable characters."
Lancashire Evening Post

"A rising star in historical fiction."
The Bookseller

"A writer who sweeps you up and carries you along."
Andy Shepherd

"Stunningly atmospheric."
Polly Ho-Yen

"A thrilling tale of secrets, sisters and power gone wrong."
Judith Eagle

"Atmospheric and intriguing."
South Wales Evening Post

D0785079

30118142546104

Lancashire Library Services	
30118142546104	
PETERS	JF
£7.99	24-Sep-2021
SCH	

For Mum and Dad

First published in the UK in 2021 by Usborne Publishing Ltd., Usborne House, 83-85 Saffron Hill, London EC1N 8RT, England, usborne.com.

Usborne Verlag, Usborne Publishing Ltd., Prüfeninger Str. 20, 93049 Regensburg, Deutschland VK Nr. 17560

Copyright © Ann-Marie Howell, 2021.

The right of Ann-Marie Howell to be identified as the author of this work has been asserted by her in accordance with the Copyright, Designs and Patents Act, 1988.

Cover, inside illustrations and map by Saara Katariina Söderlund © Usborne Publishing, 2021.

Border © Lena Pan / Shutterstock.

Photo of Ann-Marie Howell © Nick Ilott Photography, 2019.

The name Usborne and the Balloon logo are Trade Marks of Usborne Publishing Ltd.

All rights reserved. No part of this publication may be reproduced, stored in a retrieval system or transmitted in any form or by any means, electronic, mechanical, photocopying, recording or otherwise without the prior permission of the publisher.

This is a work of fiction. The characters, incidents, and dialogues are products of the author's imagination and are not to be construed as real. Any resemblance to actual events or persons, living or dead, is entirely coincidental.

A CIP catalogue record for this book is available from the British Library.

ISBN: 9781474991063 07141/1 JFMA JJASOND/21

Printed and bound in Great Britain by CPI Group (UK) Ltd, Croydon, CR0 4YY.

MIX
Paper from
responsible sources
FSC® C020471

MYSTERY
of the
NIGHT
WATCHERS

A. M. HOWELL

USBORNE

Contents

Botanic Gardens

NORTHGATE STREET

Abbey Gate

ANGEL HILL

Cavendish's Haberdashery

CAVENDISH'S haberdashery

LOOMS LANE

Thurlow Champness

THURLOW CHAMPNESS

ABBEYGATE STREET

HIGH BAXTER STREET

MARKET

BUTTER

Cupola House

THE TRAVERSE

TO THE POLICE STATION

While much of Bury has been brought to life here as it would have been in 1910, a few small changes have been made in the interest of the story. You can read more about these changes at the back of the book.

CHAPTER I

Anything But Normal

It was not normal for Nancy to see her mother's pale cheeks tilted towards the night sky in their back garden as they had been for the past week, watching for the return of Halley's comet. It was not normal for Nancy to come across her mother cleaning their family's shoes two nights in a row after everyone had retired to bed, her long nightgown covered in thumbprint smudges of black polish. Nancy also felt it was far from normal for her mother to be so mesmerized by the unremarkable table clock in the hallway of their Leeds town house, staring at it in the way you might do just before a birthday or Christmas, eager for time to march onwards.

When Nancy questioned her mother about these things, she would just give her a distracted smile and set her a task, like folding ironed clothes, helping her younger sister Violet perfect the curves of her handwriting on her school slate, or taking their terrier Monty for a walk.

But these strange things Nancy noticed about her mother had settled in her mind, making her alert for other strange behaviour. Which is why Nancy was staring hard at her mother now as she bustled about clearing away teacups and saucers and kipper-smeared breakfast plates. Mrs Bell, their home help, normally came in to do this after she and Violet had gone to school.

Knowing that she was unlikely to get a satisfactory answer to why her mother was behaving like this, Nancy sighed, left the kitchen and walked into the hall to say goodbye to her father as he prepared to go to work. She brushed past Violet, who was sitting on the bottom step of the stairs feeding an already portly Monty the remains of her breakfast sausage, her school socks around her ankles, a smear of brown sauce staining the sleeve of her white school blouse.

"Goodbye, Father. And good luck today," Nancy said, passing him his black hat and umbrella from the coat stand.

Her father's forehead crinkled into a frown as he adjusted his hat and bent to give Nancy a quick kiss on the cheek. "I'll do my best. I know you think the punishment is harsh, but theft is a serious crime, no matter what the circumstances."

Nancy pushed her hands into the pockets of her navy-blue school pinafore, thinking that while her father as a solicitor had to respect the law at all times, it would be most unfair if the children in his case today were sent to prison for stealing a few apples. They were only hungry after all.

Her mother rushed down the hallway, wiping her hands on her apron. "It worries me that you take your father's court cases to heart so, Nancy," she said, passing him a fresh handkerchief from a drawer in the sideboard.

"It worries me too, dear. It worries me a great deal," said Nancy's father, pushing the handkerchief into his trouser pocket and putting on his mackintosh. "Not that Nancy takes my cases to heart, but that these boys at fourteen – just two years older than she is – should have their young lives take such a terrible turn for the worse. You should be proud of our daughter for having such a strong moral compass. I know that I am."

"Do I have your moral compass too, Father?" piped up Violet, lifting up Monty and kissing his wriggling ears.

Nancy's father did up the last brown button of his mackintosh and smiled. "Yes, little darling. I am certain of it."

Nancy looked up at her father, and then at Violet and saw how alike they were with their amber-flecked eyes. Nancy might have the same moral compass as her father, but she hadn't inherited his eye colour. Her birth father had died when she was just one. With no remaining family in Suffolk, Mother had told her that a year later she had packed up their things and moved to Leeds, with Nancy in one hand and a single suitcase in the other, to lodge with an old family friend. She had soon met and married Jacob, and Nancy's half-sister Violet had arrived a few years later.

After kissing their father goodbye and closing the front door behind him, Nancy's mother glanced at the table clock ticking on the sideboard. "Come along, girls. We don't want to be late for school," she said.

"But it's still early, we don't need to leave yet," said Nancy, also looking at the clock. Her mother was in her peculiar mood again, just as she had been all week.

"Violet, your blouse," fretted their mother, noticing the stain and looking at her youngest daughter in dismay. "Nancy, please help Violet find a clean one upstairs."

"But…" Nancy started to protest.

"Now, please, Nancy," said Mother in a voice that meant business.

"I can find it on my own," piped up Violet.

"No, your sister will help. Off you go. I expect you both to be downstairs in five minutes with your coats, hats and shoes on," said their mother firmly, taking off her apron, smoothing the fabric of her long, dove-grey skirt and adjusting the enamel brooch at the neck of her blouse.

Nancy sighed and looked down at her little sister, her dark wayward hair and pink cheeks. She raised her fingers to her own walnut-brown, shoulder-length curls that were neatly braided, and reminded herself that Violet was only seven and could not be expected to do everything by herself, no matter how much Nancy might wish for it.

"Why is Mother in such a hurry today?" Violet asked, as they traipsed upstairs.

"I have no idea," sighed Nancy. "I have a mathematics test at school and I certainly don't want to be early for that!"

The drizzle dulled everything to grey as Mother hurried Nancy and Violet along on their twenty-minute route to school. Nancy tightened the ribbons on the straw hat that she wore day in day out, now that spring had supposedly arrived, and walked ahead, enjoying the distance from Violet, who chattered incessantly. She strode past the greengrocer's, admiring the arrangement of imported pineapples and mandarins in the window, past the newspaper boy on the corner who tipped his cap to her and bellowed, "Halley's comet...get your latest news here." She stood for a second and looked at the headlines on the front of his stand.

* FRIDAY 13TH MAY 1910 *

NATION CONTINUES TO MOURN
THE DEATH OF KING EDWARD VII.

FEARS OF HALLEY'S COMET ARE FOOLISH AND UNFOUNDED!

Every evening for the past month Nancy had been scouring her father's copy of the *Leeds Mercury* newspaper for articles about Halley's comet, which was due to pass by the Earth after an absence of seventy-five years. Advances in science meant that this time the presence of a toxic cyanogen gas in the comet's tail had been detected. Her father had explained that this in itself was not thought to be a problem, but as the Earth was due to travel directly through the comet's tail in less than a week's time, there had been some talk that the gas would be deadly to humankind. The closer the comet got to Earth, the clearer it became, and for the past week Nancy had watched for it from her bedroom window, wondering if she should be worried about it. For some scientists were telling people to stay indoors, seal up their windows, wear protective gas masks and take preventative anti-comet pills to stop themselves from being poisoned. Nancy knew her father was firmly of the opinion that the comet would cause no ill effects and anticipated its arrival keenly, but she noticed her mother's cheeks would become drawn and pale when anyone spoke of the comet. This caused a glimmer of unease to rise in Nancy's chest and she wondered whether her mother perhaps had a different view that she was keeping to herself. Could that be why she had been standing in the garden looking at the night sky a little fearfully?

Nancy nodded to the paperboy and strode past two women wearing the fashionable hobble skirts that her mother despised so, preferring more fluid skirts and dresses instead. ("They are called hobble skirts for a reason, Nancy," she would say. "I will not have my stride restricted by such a ridiculous garment.") Omnibuses rumbled by, passengers packed like sardines on their way into the city for a day of work. Motor cars occasionally overtook the buses – there were more on the roads than ever and her father had even said quite casually the week before that he had been wondering whether they should buy one. Leeds became as hot and smoky as a factory chimney in the summer and it would be nice to drive to the coast and take in the sea air more frequently.

Nancy was so distracted by her thoughts of gently lapping waves between her toes, that she realized she had passed their usual turning to the school. But when she looked behind, she saw their mother had also missed the turn and was marching straight ahead with a determined look on her face. Violet was pulling on Mother's arm.

Nancy came to a halt and waited. "We missed the turn," she said. It was then that she noticed their mother was clutching something in her left hand. A moss-green carpet bag. "What's that?" she asked, her nose wrinkling.

Mother gave Nancy a quick glance. "We're going away for a few days."

Nancy stared.

"Does that mean no school?" said Violet with a grin. "Hurrah."

"What do you mean, *going away*?" asked Nancy. She looked at the carpet bag again. Caught between the bag's clasp was the hem of her best cream nightgown. She swallowed. "But I have a mathematics test at school and—"

"There will be no mathematics test – in fact there will be no school for either of you today, or the early part of next week," their mother interrupted, adjusting her grey felt hat. "We are going on a journey and I need you both to be very well behaved and not ask too many questions. Now, the omnibus stop we need to take us to the train station is just over there."

Nancy frowned. A *train* journey on a school day? She watched Mother take Violet's hand and march onwards. Nancy looked back in the direction of her school, a jolt of unease tightening her throat. This was anything but normal. Why would their mother suggest such a trip and where was she taking them?

CHAPTER 2

Train Station

Nancy gripped Violet's hand firmly, the smell of oil and smoke smarting in her nose, the occasional train whistle blasting, as they hurried to keep up with their mother, who was moving quickly through the station.

"Keep close, my darlings," their mother said, turning briefly to glance at her children, her gloved fingers clenched around the leather handle of the carpet bag. The sight of the bag again brought Nancy to a sudden halt, as bursts of steam punctured the air, the trains groaning as they pulled in and out of Leeds station.

Their mother paused, looked up at a large clock overhead and shook her head a little. "Come on, girls. We mustn't miss this train. Nancy...Violet...are you listening?"

Nancy *was* listening, and while she had to obey her mother's instructions, because that was just the way things were, she also did not want to move an inch until she knew why they were going on this unexpected journey.

Porters pushing carts loaded with travelling trunks, men clutching black umbrellas and smartly dressed couples holding overnight bags bustled past, as their mother turned and plonked the carpet bag down. A man wiping his steamed-up spectacles stumbled into them. Mother ignored his tut of annoyance and gave her daughters a gentle smile. "I realize it is unusual to be taking a train on a May Friday, and a school day at that. But...well... we are going to stay with your grandfather for a while."

Violet slipped her hand from Nancy's. Nancy wiped her sweaty palm on her beige coat, wondering why they must visit their grandfather now.

"Whoopee!" Violet said, her eyes shining. "Can I feed the fish in his pond? He said we could build a tree house the next time we came to visit."

Their mother pressed her lips together into a paper-thin line, then dragged in a breath. "No, Violet. We're not going to see Grandpa in York. Oh, do watch where you are going!" she hissed at a couple who were so preoccupied giving each other lovey-dovey looks they too almost tripped over the carpet bag. Nancy leaned forward and picked it up. The weight of it caused her to sway a little.

"We're going to stay with your other grandfather," Mother said, the words slipping from her mouth as quick as a waterfall.

Nancy and Violet exchanged puzzled glances.

"But we don't *have* another grandfather," said Nancy slowly. "You told us that both of your parents died when you were young."

Mother looked down at her shoes. "My mother died, but my father is still alive. You do have another grandfather after all."

"Does he have fish?" asked Violet hopefully, hopping from foot to foot, seemingly unaware of the enormity of this new piece of information their mother had just told them.

"*You do after all,*" echoed Nancy, taking a step closer to her mother. "What does *that* mean?" How could she have kept this a secret from them? Their father didn't like secrets and said they were the cause of many troubles in the world. So why had their mother chosen to lie about something as important as this?

Mother ignored Nancy's question, glanced at the clock again, sighed and pulled three train tickets from her coat pocket. "The ten o'clock from Leeds to Peterborough, then a few changes to get us across the country to Suffolk. Off we go. Please, darlings – do keep up!" She snatched the carpet bag from Nancy and began pushing her way through the crowds.

Nancy grabbed Violet's hand again and hurried on, sweat trickling uncomfortably down her back as they were bustled into a second-class compartment on the Peterborough-bound train, steam from beneath the wheels snapping at their heels. Their mother's cheeks were pink with exertion, strands of hair escaping from her neatly pinned bun. She pushed the carpet bag into the luggage rack above the seats and then stood at the window rubbing her arms as if she had a chill.

"Does our new grandfather have a tree we could build a house in?" asked Violet, jumping onto the seat and clinging to the strings of the luggage rack like a monkey.

"Violet, get down," said Nancy, tugging on her arm.

Their mother was so distracted she hadn't even noticed Violet was standing on the train seat, but a woman and man entering the compartment most certainly had and gave her a disapproving stare.

"Please can you put my gas mask up on the luggage rack, Arthur?" asked the woman with hair the colour of Mother's best silver cutlery.

Nancy stared at the square brown box which the woman passed to her equally silver-haired husband. She shifted her gaze to Violet and lifted her off the seat, plonking her on the floor. "What about Father?" she asked. "Does he know where we're going?"

Mother sat on the edge of the seat, placed her hands on her lap and peeled off her leather gloves. "I have left him a note telling him all he needs to know and that we will return by the middle of next week. Mrs Bell will bring him his meals, make the bed and look after Monty."

Nancy frowned. It sounded as if this trip had been planned for a while. Was this why their mother had been behaving so strangely for the past week?

"My father…your grandfather is…unwell," Mother said, talking under her breath, while glancing at their compartment companions as if afraid she would be overheard. "He is a keen astronomer and requires help viewing Halley's comet. That is all you need to know for now. I will need your help, Nancy, in looking after your sister. Please try and occupy her while we are there." She paused for a second and looked at Violet, who was now kneeling on the seat beside her with her nose to the window. The guard blew his whistle and the train began to pull away from the platform. "We'll return home when the view of the comet has started to wane. And don't worry about school. I informed them that you and Violet would be absent for a few days," Mother continued, settling Violet properly in her seat.

A wave of heat rose up Nancy's back. "You told them? When?"

"Yesterday," her mother said, fiddling with her thin gold wedding ring.

Yesterday. Was that why the headmistress had pulled her to one side while they were writing the countries of Europe on their slates and asked if everything was all right at home? Of course Nancy had said yes, for she had thought everything *was* all right. But in the space of a day she had learned that things were not all right whatsoever and it was making her feel as unsteady as the train, as it juddered and rocked its way out of the station.

The elderly couple had sat down opposite them and began unwrapping sandwiches in brown paper. The tangy smell of pickle filled the compartment. The man glanced up at Nancy's mother. "Got gas masks for your little ones, have you? Did you see the report in the paper yesterday? This comet with its gassy tail will be the end of us all. We're off to stay with my sister. We should be together at a time like this."

The woman threw her husband a disapproving look. "Shush. You don't want to upset the children," she whispered.

Nancy thought of Mother in their garden at night watching the sky. She had said their grandfather was unwell and needed help to view the comet. Was that the real reason they were going to Suffolk, or was it so that their mother could be reunited with her *own* father before time ran out and the deadly gas from the comet's tail poisoned them all? Did that mean that Mother thought the scientists were right and her father wrong? Nancy slumped back in her seat. She really did not know what to believe and she did not understand why Mother was acting this way. She wondered, with trepidation, what lay in wait for them at the end of their long train journey.

CHAPTER 3

Silver Smudge

The elderly couple opposite spent the first part of their journey to Peterborough trying to engage Nancy, Violet and their mother in various and wide-ranging topics of conversation.

"It's a strange time, what with the death of King Edward only a week back. Some superstitious folk are saying the arrival of the comet could have killed the king – what do you think?" asked the man, looking at Nancy and taking a bite from a juicy red apple.

"Oh. My father said the king had a bad heart," said Nancy with a frown, wishing her mother would participate in the conversation. But she was looking pointedly out of the window.

"What does your father do?"

"Why are you not at school today?"

"Are you sealing up your windows and doors against the gas?"

"Do you have some anti-comet pills to protect against the poison?"

Upon asking this question, the man's wife sucked in a breath and nudged him in the side, at the same time as their mother turned back from the window, her eyes quite saucer-like. "My children are young and impressionable and I would appreciate it if these questions would stop."

Nancy almost gasped at their mother's brittle tone and glanced anxiously at Violet, but she was oblivious, fast asleep with her head lolling to one side. Nancy slipped her hands under her legs and pressed her fingers into the springy seat-cushion. It was most unlike their mother to be so abrupt with strangers. Mother's cheeks were flushed, her hands gripping her knees as she turned away again to look out of the window. An awkward silence settled on the compartment as the train puffed through countryside peppered with grazing sheep and cows.

Mother eventually rummaged in her handbag and pulled out a piece of cloth. "Here, you can get on with your needlework," she said, passing Nancy a plain white handkerchief and a length of red satin ribbon for the edging. She and her mother made the handkerchiefs to support the efforts of the local Women's Suffrage Society, a group which campaigned peacefully for changes in women's rights. Nancy threaded her needle and began to work on her handkerchief as they headed south, leaving the last of the damp weather behind and travelling into the type of spring she had read about in books, where birds swooped and dived in an endless blue sky, crops pushed up through the soil and everything seemed fresh and new.

"We've arrived. Come on, girls, hurry now," Nancy's mother said in a low voice as the slow screech of the train's brakes filled the carriage.

Nancy pulled herself upright and massaged the crick in her neck. Her mouth was sour from the fish paste sandwiches her mother had given them for lunch and tea, her eyes gritty with tiredness after travelling all day. Violet yawned, stood up slowly and stretched. The girls alighted from the train, along with a few other weary-looking passengers, into a small red-brick station, with none of the hustle and bustle of Leeds or Peterborough. The dim lights on the platform flickered.

Nancy glanced at the black hands of the station clock overhead. It was a little after nine o'clock in the evening. "Is he coming to meet us?" she asked, as their mother began to march along the platform into the gloom.

"Who?" Mother asked.

"Grandfather," said Nancy.

"I told you, darling, he's unwell," said their mother, adjusting the tilt of her hat.

The guard blew on his whistle and the train began to hiss and steam and pull away.

"Come along, we'll walk to the house," Mother said, leading them to the station entrance and past two waiting hansom cabs, the horses snorting and stamping their feet, the air ripe with the smell of fresh dung.

"But I'm tired," complained Violet.

With a sigh, Mother put the carpet bag down. "Girls, there is something you must do for me while we are here." Her face was ghostly in the low light.

Nancy stared at her mother, feeling a pinch of unease at what she might be about to say.

"Apart from the fact that I need you to be very good and quiet, we all need to stay inside the house and not be seen." She said this in a very matter-of-fact way, as if it was an ordinary request.

Nancy looked at her mother with confusion. "What do you mean 'not be seen'?"

"Why do we have to stay inside?" asked Violet, wrinkling her nose.

Mother glanced up and down the quiet street. She pressed a hand to her chest. "I fear that this is too much to ask of you, my dears."

"Why must we stay in?" asked Violet again. "Can't we even go to a park?"

Mother looked at them both. "No, you cannot. I need you both to do as I ask, and not question my decisions while we are here."

Nancy swallowed the lump that sat in her throat as firm as a hard-boiled egg. The worries in her life up until now, usually about school or a disagreement with a friend, suddenly seemed quite small in comparison to what had happened today. Night seemed to have fallen suddenly, cloaking them in darkness. "Yes, of course we'll do as you say, Mother," she said quickly, her toes curling uncomfortably in her black school shoes.

Violet's shoulders drooped and their mother led them away from the station and up a hill towards the lights of the town. Was it Nancy's imagination, or was their mother avoiding the glow of the electric street lamps? Nancy shivered, at that moment wanting nothing more than to be inside, away from the darkness and gathering shadows.

"Look, Mother. Is that…the comet?" whispered Violet after a short while, pointing to the inky sky.

Nancy followed her sister's pointing finger to a silver smudge between two stars, a little like a thumbnail that had been blurred around the edges. It was just like the artists' impressions she had seen in the *Leeds Mercury* newspaper.

Her mother tipped her head upwards too, her eyes unreadable. "Yes, it is."

"Are you afraid of the comet, Mother?" asked Nancy quietly. "Do you think the gas in its tail will harm us?"

Her mother shook her head. "No. I'm not afraid of the comet, and you shouldn't be either," she said in a small, fierce voice.

Nancy looked at her in surprise. This was not the answer she had perhaps been expecting. While it was reassuring to know that the reason for their visit had nothing to do with Mother being afraid of the comet, her decision to bring them here now and the instructions for her and Violet to stay inside and be unseen were very unnerving. Nancy's world had tilted a little and she wished for nothing more than to push it back into place. Their mother looked at the comet for a few seconds more, before marching onwards in silence.

Nancy stared and stared at the silver smudge, until it was consumed by a cloud and it was as if the comet had never been there at all.

CHAPTER 4

Cupola House

"We're almost there," Mother said in a low voice as they trod quietly over cobbles, past a butchery and grocery with shuttered windows and the town fire station, the soft whinny of a horse coming from under its stable doors. She came to a halt in front of a wide cream-painted building, jars of brightly coloured liquids glinting in its two curved bay windows. Mother shifted the carpet bag into her left hand, looked quickly behind her as if checking that no one was watching, then walked up the three steps to the shop door and waited. Nancy felt a growing anticipation as she stood outside this new and unfamiliar place.

Violet ran after Mother, the soles of her shoes slapping on the stone.

"Hush," Mother whispered, frowning at Violet.

Nancy looked up at the building and spotted a small balcony jutting from the third floor. Above this she saw the slope of the roof, some attic windows, and something unexpected. She stepped back to get a better look, her jaw dropping in awe. A small octagonal turret sat on the very top of the roof; a flash of moonlight illuminating its small arched windows. The view from up there must be quite tremendous. Was this where their grandfather observed the comet?

"Nancy," hissed their mother.

Nancy ran lightly up the steps to the shop and waited behind Violet. In the dim light she saw a nameplate attached to the wall of the building. *Cupola House*. She bit on her lower lip and looked at the bell pull. Wasn't Mother going to use it? But there was no need, for the door opened a second later, as if whoever was inside had been fully expecting them to arrive at that very moment.

Mother slipped through the half-open door, beckoning for them to follow. Violet reached for

Nancy's hand, her fingers damp. Nancy held her sister's hand tight, suddenly nervous about meeting their new grandfather.

A dim light and an infusion of smells greeted them as they stepped into the shop: floral soaps, exotic herbs and spices and the metallic odour of oils and vinegars. Nancy breathed deeply as she looked at the small man with neat greying hair, a clipped moustache and gold-rimmed spectacles, who was clasping their mother's gloved hands tightly between his. "Charlotte. My dearest girl. I never…I never…expected to…"

"Shush, Father," Mother said firmly. She loosened her hands from his grasp and closed the door behind Nancy and Violet, turned the key, then placed it on the shop counter. "Before you say anything, you must understand I had no choice but to bring the children." There was a catch in Mother's voice and Nancy noticed a tremor in her hand as she fiddled with the buttons on her gloves. "Violet, Nancy, please say hello to your grandfather."

Their new grandfather looked at Nancy and Violet with wide-eyed alarm, a frown puckering his forehead. He looked back at their mother. "You should have come alone," he said.

"I know what your letter asked me to do," said their mother finally, taking off her gloves. "But their father could not be expected to look after them. I have told the girls they must stay in the house while we are here and not be seen."

Nancy looked at her mother curiously. She had been receiving letters from their grandfather, which made it even stranger that they didn't know he was alive and had never met him before.

Their grandfather's frown deepened. "Well, I suppose they are here now and there is nothing to be done about it." He took a tentative step towards Violet and shook her hand, in the manner you might greet someone at an important business meeting. Violet grinned, but he didn't return her smile. "She has a touch of you about her, Charlotte," he said gruffly. He turned to Nancy and looked her up and down, as if assessing her suitability for an important task. "Well," he said again. His eyes suddenly became watery. He pulled a large (and rather dirty-looking) handkerchief from his pocket and blew his nose noisily, then pushed it back into his pocket. He clasped Nancy's hands between his. His knuckles were as gnarly as tree bark, but his palms were soft and cool. "You're still the girl I once knew, but how you've grown. I'm pleased to make your acquaintance again, Nancy." A flush spread up Grandfather's neck and he gave their mother a quick glance, as if checking to see that had been the correct thing to say.

"Um. It's nice to meet you too," said Nancy, wondering exactly *when* she and her grandfather had last seen each other.

"I have told the girls we have come to help you watch the comet," their mother said. She seemed suddenly bowed with weariness from the journey and their arrival.

"Ah, yes, the comet. It will be quite a sight," said their grandfather slowly, pushing his spectacles onto his nose.

Nancy glanced around, as a steady silence settled over them and the shop. Her eyes flitted to the gold-labelled jars and bottles stacked on the wooden shelves behind the counter and the rows of miniature drawers below them, the glass-fronted cabinets containing toothbrushes, tobacco and different types of vinegar and antacid remedies. She glanced at the wooden sign above the door etched with faded gold lettering. *Laurence Greenstone. Licensed Apothecary.* Her grandfather was a man who prepared and sold medicines.

Grandfather followed her gaze. "This shop and the house above it have belonged to the Greenstone family for generations." He lay a hand on a glass cabinet and looked at the contents in a proud and protective manner, as if they were eggs in a nest. "I hope it will stay in our family for many more years to come." He glanced at Nancy's mother and something unsaid seemed to pass between them.

As Nancy continued to look around, she realized that when her mother was a girl she must have stood in this very shop as her grandfather worked, grinding and selling herbs and potions and remedies to cure all manner of illnesses and ailments. Perhaps that was why she was always so skilled in knowing how to treat a grazed knee or an insect bite.

"Come on, girls. Bedtime," their mother said. "It's been a long journey for us all."

"Nancy and Violet can sleep in your old room on the first floor," their grandfather said. "It will mean we don't disturb them when we are watching the comet and I am sure they will appreciate each other's company." Grandfather and Mother looked at each other steadily, as if again thoughts were transferring between them on a telegraph wire.

"Am I going to sleep in your bed, Mother?" Violet asked. "The one you slept in when you were small?"

Their mother smiled a weary smile. "I believe you might, darling."

Nancy's heart sank at the thought of sharing a room with Violet. She had only recently moved into a small third-floor box room at home, cherishing the quiet space away from her sister's boundless energy. It would be tiresome to share.

She followed her mother and grandfather around the shop counter and through a door that led into a square hallway, where a thick oak staircase wound upwards through the house like an angular snake. On a table at the foot of the stairs stood a huddle of brass-footed oil lamps. Her grandfather pulled a box of matches from his jacket pocket and carefully lit the wicks of three lamps, passing one to their mother, one to Nancy and picking the final one up himself.

"Why do we need these?" asked Nancy, thinking about the electric lights her father had paid a fitter to install at their home in Leeds a few years ago, replacing their old gas lamps.

"I'm afraid oil provides the only source of light in

this house," said Grandfather, the stairs creaking and groaning as he began to climb.

Nancy frowned. She had seen street lamps on the way from the station, so electricity had clearly arrived in this small town. "But don't you even have gas lamps?" she asked.

"I'm afraid I'm a little behind the times. There's been no money to spend on the house, but it's comfortable enough for my needs," Grandfather replied.

The flame inside the pink frosted glass of the lamp wavered as Nancy followed her grandfather and mother up the stairs. Oil lamps were very old-fashioned. Positively Victorian! Nancy had quickly grown used to flicking a wall switch to turn on a light and could not imagine being without electricity, even if the supply wasn't completely reliable and they occasionally had to resort to candles when there were unexpected outages.

Violet shuddered as they trod past a gargoyle carved into the wooden staircase. It gazed at them mischievously, its lips curved in mirth. The gargoyle was a little creepy, but something else was unsettling Nancy, a distinctive earthy smell that was growing stronger and more pungent as they followed their grandfather's steady steps up into the heart of the house.

Stepping out onto the large first-floor landing, Nancy gasped.

"Cripes," whispered Violet.

The scene in front of them was not at all what Nancy had expected from the house as they had stood outside it. She looked at her new grandfather curiously, wondering if this was a sign that he was not quite what he seemed from the outside either.

Chapter 5

Peculiarities

Plants in terracotta pots of varying sizes jostled for space across the landing, crammed onto a wall-to-wall Persian rug. There were small plants with fine green leaves, larger plants with tall greyish stems, squat plants with delicate fronds, all of them filling the air with a heady fragrance. A tall window stretched up in front of them, and to the right of it was a wooden shelf containing glass jars and bottles in which leaves and flowers were suspended in a clear, oily liquid.

"It's like an indoor garden," said Nancy, glancing at her mother, who was stiff and pale-faced as she looked around, the oil lamp shaking a little in her hand.

Grandfather placed his lamp on a table, bent down and plucked a leaf from one of the smaller plants. He held it to his nose and sniffed. "I grow these herbs to make remedies, not that there's any call for them now. But tending to my plants keeps me busy – makes me feel useful."

Nancy's mother gave a small shake of her head and bit on her bottom lip. "You used to grow these outside the shop every spring and summer, right by the front door…" Her voice trailed off.

"I cannot do that any more," their grandfather replied, pressing the leaf between a finger and thumb.

"Why not?" asked Nancy, thinking that it did seem a little peculiar to be growing so many herbs indoors.

Grandfather crushed the leaf between his forefinger and thumb, then pulled out his handkerchief and briskly wiped his hands. It seemed Nancy was not to get an answer to her question. The grown-ups exchanged another look which was hiding something Nancy could not interpret.

"Why are there leaves inside these jars?" asked Violet, who was peering at the shelf.

"They are herbal oils," their grandfather replied,

"to help cure aches and pains."

"They're pretty. Can I look at them?" asked Violet, stretching out her fingers towards them.

"Not now," said their mother.

"Perhaps another time," said their grandfather softly, giving her a small smile.

"Come along, Violet. It really is time for bed," said their mother, taking Violet's hand and leading her away from the shelves towards a door to the left of the window.

"On this floor is the drawing room, library and two more bedrooms," Grandfather said to Nancy. "Your room overlooks The Traverse – that's the name of the street outside the shop."

Nancy looked at the winding staircase which continued to the floors above, and thought of the octagonal structure on the roof she had seen when they first arrived. "Do you watch the comet from the room on the roof?" she asked her grandfather curiously.

Grandfather nodded. "It's called a cupola – a small observatory. You can see for miles from up there." His voice had a sad edge to it, as if this didn't make him very happy. Nancy thought this was also a little peculiar, for surely a view for miles was exactly what he *would* want from a rooftop observatory. She gave her grandfather a cautious smile and was about to follow her mother and sister into the bedroom when he placed a gentle hand on her arm. "I'm afraid the cupola is out of bounds to you and Violet. I have an antique telescope in there; it is delicate and could easily be broken."

"Yes, Grandfather," Nancy said quickly. It felt a little strange to call him that when they had only just met.

He let his hand drop to his side and his face relaxed into a warm smile. Beckoning her to follow, he disappeared into the bedroom after Mother and Violet.

Nancy drew in a breath. *Be quiet, stay inside the house, don't go into the cupola.* Helping their grandfather view the comet was the reason for their visit, so it was a little confusing that they were not allowed in his observatory. The rules they must keep while staying in this house were plentiful.

Stepping after Grandfather into her mother's childhood bedroom, Nancy half expected to be greeted by an abundance of greenery and sweet-smelling herbs, but was instead confronted by an old-fashioned, vibrantly decorated room. The cream wallpaper was laced with exotic gold birds and butterflies which danced among twisted branches. The wooden floorboards were thick with dust that gathered around the bed legs like fluffy grey mice. A washstand with a white porcelain bowl stood in one corner and the open door of a heavy wooden wardrobe revealed an empty interior. Two single dark-wood beds and chests of drawers sat next to the longest walls facing the two windows, where the droopy jade-green brocade curtains had provided a feast for a hungry moth or two.

The fustiness of the room made Nancy place the oil lamp on the table and slump onto the nearest bed. It seemed that this room had been uninhabited for so long the dust and wood were attempting to claim the house as their own. Had this really been her mother's room when she was a girl? There was no evidence of her, no dolls or books or anything to make it feel loved. She patted the pillow and coughed as dust motes danced and leaped. She had a suspicion it may not have been washed since her mother was a child.

Violet bounded over to the bed on the other side of the room and jumped on it. "You had two beds to sleep in, Mother," she said.

Their mother stood by the closed curtains, a frown straining her features. "Yes. Another bed for when a friend came to stay."

Nancy watched the dust motes swirl around Violet as the bed creaked in time with her bounces.

Their grandfather gave an apologetic shrug which lifted his shirt collar to his pink ears. "Sorry about the dust. Not had any visitors…since…well." He rubbed his chin.

"Never mind," said their mother briskly. "We'll soon get things shipshape." She lifted the pillows and patted the worst of the dust from them, then did the same with the blankets. "Take your nightdresses from the bag, girls. I'll bring you some warm water for the washstand and a commode each."

Nancy stared at her mother, her mouth falling open. "A commode? Isn't there a flushing toilet?"

"You won't find all of the furnishings and fittings you are used to here," said Mother, glancing at their grandfather. He gave them another small, limp shrug.

Nancy thought of their bathroom suite at home, the flushing toilet which clanked like a turning wheel when you pulled the chain, the bath edged in wood and matching sink with brass taps. She knew they were lucky to have those facilities, for her father had told her that the poorer people he represented in court had no indoor bathroom and shared an outdoor toilet with several other houses on their street. That was proper hardship. Nancy sighed. They were only to stay here for a few days to help their grandfather. She needed to buckle down and make the best of it.

After Nancy had washed and said goodnight to her mother, and pushed the porcelain-lidded commode under her bed, she turned the oil lamp down to a low flicker and lay listening to the evenness of Violet's breathing as she slept. Her legs felt leaden with tiredness, but her head was still buzzing from everything that had happened that day. Mother had left their father a note, but what had it said? Did he know of their grandfather's existence? She felt sure he hadn't known of their trip to Suffolk in advance, or else he would have mentioned it when saying goodbye that morning. Her stomach twisted into a hard little knot as she imagined him sitting in the parlour with only Monty for company. She shifted in bed, pushing the musty blanket away from her nose. Grandfather seemed a little wistful, but he was someone she could imagine liking in time. Something was niggling at her, though, something about him.

She sat up in bed in a dizzying rush. She thought of her grandfather's even breathing, the slow but steady way he trod up the stairs, the way he bent to pick a leaf from the potted herb. *He was elderly, but he didn't seem ill.* Which meant that her mother had lied about something else. If he wasn't ill, then why had they come all this way to Suffolk? Nancy occasionally wondered whether adults must think children rather stupid to believe everything they were told. But today she had realized for the first time that perhaps she should not believe *anything* that adults told her, particularly members of her own family, which was a very worrying turn of events indeed. Something peculiar was going on and she was determined to work out what.

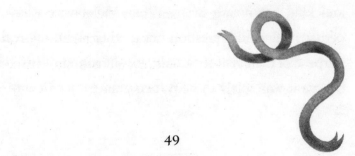

Chapter 6

Whispers

The creak of floorboards woke Nancy with a jolt. She sat up, glanced at the dim outline of Violet, watching the rise and fall of the blanket as she slept. A rim of light around the edges of the moth-ravaged curtains suggested it was early morning. Perhaps her mother was up and about already. The happenings of the previous day rushed into Nancy's head, almost knocking her breath away. While Violet was asleep, perhaps she could question her mother about the real purpose of their visit to Suffolk, for she found it hard to believe it was solely to help their grandfather view the comet due to his supposed poor health, especially as they weren't even allowed in the cupola. She wanted to know more about the odd instruction to stay inside the house too. This suggested their stay here was to be kept a secret. Why was that?

Flinging back the sheets and blanket, Nancy climbed out of bed, the wooden floorboards cool under her bare feet. She thought of her mother's feet standing on this very same spot years ago. What had she been like as a girl? Mother had never spoken of her childhood, only assuring them it had been a happy one. She was an only child, said her parents had sadly passed away when she was young. It was a painful time to think of, and that was why she never spoke of it. At least, that was the story Nancy had been told, but now she knew it was a lie.

The fact Mother had kept their grandfather from them swirled and churned in the pit of Nancy's stomach. Mother could seek out small untruths from her and Violet like a bloodhound. Learning that *she herself* was capable of telling such a large lie made Nancy feel as if a rug had been pulled sharply from beneath her feet.

Tiptoeing to the door, Nancy opened it, the gentle creak of its ancient hinges causing her to pause and listen. Violet did not stir, but as Nancy crept from the room onto the wide plant-filled landing she could hear the sound of whispered voices coming from above. *Her mother and grandfather.*

The curtains were closed on the landing, but the window was slightly ajar and the leaves of the potted herbs waved gently in the early morning gloom, their fragrance wafting under Nancy's nose as she walked to the stairs and looked up. Were they still in the cupola, watching the comet? It was unlikely at this hour as it was not visible during the day. But the thought of what they might be seeing from the small rooftop observatory caused a pinch of curiosity that drew her up the stairs.

The light spilling down the stairwell grew steadily brighter, the eyes of another gnarly faced gargoyle seeming to follow Nancy's progress as she wound her way ever upwards. She winced as the stairs moaned gently in time with her footsteps, until she finally stepped out onto a small landing leading to some attic rooms. The ceiling was so low here she could reach up and graze it with her fingertips. She saw that a final, narrower and twisting staircase led towards the source of light coming down the stairs. *This must be the way to the cupola.* The voices she could hear were louder now, and Nancy hovered at the foot of the stairs, her toes curled into the floorboards.

"I told you we would see nothing," she heard her grandfather say.

"We must send a message," said her mother.

"But I have tried doing just that and received no reply," said her grandfather, his voice low and anxious.

"Then I must try," said Mother firmly. "There must be a reason the messages are being ignored." There was a short silence and Nancy wondered what messages they were talking about. "You are grey with exhaustion, Father. Must you open the shop today?" continued her mother.

"I must open up, for maybe today will be different and I shall have some customers," said her grandfather wearily.

"I cannot believe how bad things are. This has been going on for long enough," Mother replied in a small, fierce voice.

The light coming down the stairwell suddenly faded, as if a cloud had scudded across it. Nancy looked up, saw with alarm her mother's stockinged feet coming down the stairs. There was no time to run back to her bedroom, and even if she did, her mother would hear the creaks of the floorboards and know she had been lurking and listening to their private conversation. Glancing behind, Nancy saw that a door to one of the attic rooms was ajar. She ran over to it and slipped inside, her heart hammering so loudly she felt sure her mother and grandfather would be able to hear it as they passed. But their footsteps continued on down to the floor below. Leaning back against the wall, Nancy took in her new surroundings, her eyes widening as she realized that this was no ordinary attic room.

CHAPTER 7

The Cot

Nancy looked around the small attic in surprise. She had found herself in a room decorated with rosebud wallpaper, the early morning light spilling through two square windows that jutted out from the pitched roof. Much of the furniture in the room had been covered in dust sheets, but against a wall one item of furniture stood exposed, the dust sheet crumpled on the floor by its feet – a wooden cot, with slatted sides and solid ends.

Nancy walked over to it, noticing that the bedsheets and a pink crocheted blanket were tucked into the mattress, as if waiting for a small child to climb into it. Nancy placed a hand on the side of the cot, a sudden sourness springing to her mouth as her eyes settled on the small cream pillowslip embroidered with sprigs of purple lavender. A name had been stitched beneath in curly pink letters. *Nancy.* Nancy picked the pillow up, tracing the word with a forefinger. *Her cot, her pillow?* There was a creak from the floor below and she spun round, the pillow clasped in her hands. She stood and listened for a few seconds, heard the creaking stop and start again. It was just her mother and grandfather moving around downstairs.

Still holding the pillow, Nancy tiptoed around the rest of the room, pulling off dust sheets to reveal the remaining furniture. A small chest of drawers containing tiny pairs of warm woollen tights and hand-knitted cardigans and bonnets. An oak wardrobe filled with small dresses – navy flannel for winter and white muslin for summer. She let her fingers trail across the soft fabrics, her head spinning. On a small table by the window lay a box of painted wooden ABC building blocks and a book titled *Merry Rhymes*. This must have been her bedroom when she and her mother had lived in Suffolk.

Nancy squeezed her eyes shut, dredging in the depths of her brain for memories to confirm her thoughts, but there were none to be found. She had never asked her mother about where they had lived in Suffolk, and to find out it had been here in this odd house was bringing a past she had never thought of vividly to life. She had to ask her mother about this. Nancy ran lightly from the room, and with a jolt of surprise saw her mother standing before her, the skin under her tired eyes like faint bruises.

"What are you doing up here?" her mother asked. "I came to check on you, and found you gone." She looked at the pillow in Nancy's hand and swallowed.

"This has my name on it," said Nancy, her pulse thudding in her ears.

Her mother's eyes flitted nervously to the open door and back to Nancy. She rubbed at her neck, seemed to be choosing her words carefully. "Yes, we lived here with your grandfather."

Curiosity was unfurling inside Nancy like a fern leaf. "You said we had no family in Suffolk and that is why we moved to Leeds after my birth father died. Why did you lie?" Nancy hugged the pillow to her chest, folded her arms round it, feeling a sense of relief at confronting her mother and saying these words out loud.

Her mother's face dropped and for a second Nancy did not recognize her as the mother she knew, but someone wary and a little afraid. "We cannot talk of this now, Nancy. Please just be the good girl that I know you are and look after Violet while we are here."

Nancy's jaw clenched. "Why can't we talk about this? Why are the drawers and wardrobe in that room full of my baby clothes? Why didn't we take them with us when we moved to Leeds?"

Nancy's mother rubbed at her neck again, which was now a mottled pink. "You would have quickly grown out of them and we did not have room in our suitcase to take all of our possessions. It was a difficult time." Her tone was matter of fact, but Nancy sensed there was more to learn.

The death of her father must have been a terrible shock. But that still did not explain why they left for Leeds, and left so many of their things behind, including a grandfather who their mother was clearly very fond of. "You are keeping things from me and I don't like it," said Nancy, unable to stop the tremble in her voice. "Why did you pretend our grandfather didn't even exist? Why have you brought us here now?"

Her mother sighed, shook her head. "It is unlike you to be impertinent, Nancy. Please get dressed and go and see if your grandfather needs any help in the shop."

"But—" protested Nancy.

"And make sure you leave the shop before it opens – you mustn't be seen," her mother interrupted. "I shall get Violet up and be downstairs shortly to make breakfast," she said firmly.

"But why…?" began Nancy again.

Her mother silenced her with a look that was usually saved for Violet and her endless questions. But Nancy had questions too, ones that needed to be answered most urgently. And as it seemed that her mother was not going to be the one to provide those answers, she would have to seek them elsewhere.

CHAPTER 8

The Mayor

After getting dressed, Nancy walked swiftly downstairs to the apothecary shop, the small pillow clutched to her chest. The discovery of the bedroom she had slept in as a baby had brought a blurry past she had rarely thought about into sharper focus, made her breathe a little faster than normal. Violet had been intrigued by the pillow and wanted to see the bedroom and cot, but then their mother had arrived and put a stop to the conversation. Mother's refusal to talk about the past was quite infuriating. Perhaps their grandfather would have the answers that Mother was unprepared to give?

Nancy opened the internal door to the shop and was surprised to see a boy talking to her grandfather by the countertop. He was as tall and thin as a willow sapling, his height only exaggerated by the forest-green overalls he was wearing. Remembering her mother's instructions to not be seen, she stepped back into the shadowy hallway and watched and waited.

"Thank you for dropping off the provisions. I don't know how I would manage without you," said Nancy's grandfather, accepting from the boy a string bag bulging with rosy apples, oranges and an assortment of paper packets.

"It's no bother, Mr Greenstone," the boy said, tucking a comma of black hair behind his ear. "Anything I can do to help; you only have to ask."

Nancy saw her grandfather's eyes were a little hazy behind his spectacles. "You're a good lad. You don't know what it means to have someone I can count on."

"Goodbye, Mr Greenstone. See you the day after tomorrow," said the boy, who Nancy thought was looking a little concerned at her grandfather's downcast face. The boy turned then, his eyes narrowing as he stared into the hallway and the spot where Nancy was waiting. Heat flashed up her neck. He had seen her. The boy looked again at her grandfather, who was examining the contents of the shopping bag, then, giving Nancy a final curious glance, he turned and left, the shop bell jangling.

The bell seemed to jolt Nancy's grandfather from his thoughts, and he sighed, placing the bag of provisions on the countertop.

Nancy walked into the shop hesitantly. "Um. Hello. Mother said I should see if you needed any help." She glanced at the myriad of coloured bottles and jars. Rose, lavender and violet soaps. Trays of wooden horsehair toothbrushes, tins of pink toothpaste, cod liver oil. The mahogany counter was so polished she could see the outline of her reflection in it. The smells of beeswax and soaps mingled softly. Everything in here was sparkling and ordered and ready to welcome. She remembered what she'd overheard her grandfather say earlier that morning about hoping to have customers. Why wouldn't the people of this town want to visit his well-stocked shop?

"What have you there?" asked her grandfather with a frown, looking at the pillow in Nancy's arms.

"Oh. I found it in one of the attic rooms. Mother said it used to be *my* room and that we lived here," said

Nancy, hoping that her grandfather would not be as closed off as her mother and speak to her about this.

Grandfather's shoulders stiffened as if a piece of string was pulling him upwards. "Your mother never speaks of your time here?"

Nancy shook her head. "She never speaks of Suffolk at all."

Grandfather nodded, as if this wasn't unexpected. "Have *you* any memories of being here?" He was staring hard at Nancy, as if he was seeking something from her.

Nancy hugged the pillow. She wished she had some memory, however vague, of their lives in this house. "I don't remember a single thing," she said a few seconds later.

The tension in her grandfather's shoulders seemed to ease and he smiled at her. "You were too young to remember." He pointed to the small wooden drawers lining the wall behind the counter. "I could do with a little help. Why don't you put the pillow down and help me refill the herb drawers? I cleaned out the old stock yesterday. It's a soothing task and perhaps we can talk a little," he said.

Nancy followed him to the storeroom where he showed her the hessian sacks of herbs. Returning to the shop, she followed his instructions on how to use a wooden scoop to transfer the herbs into the drawers. *Chamomile for sleep. Peppermint for digestion. Lemon balm and valerian for nervous disorders.* The scents were soothing and Nancy breathed deeply as she worked. Every so often she glanced at her grandfather, who was sweeping the floor, and wondered when he might speak.

"I am glad you have a kind father and a little sister," said her grandfather eventually. "Your mother was so sad after your birth father passed away."

Nancy's hand stilled over the lavender drawer. She turned and saw her grandfather was watching her with misty eyes, the broom handle tight in his fist.

Nancy placed the scoop on the counter next to the pillow, feeling a sudden lurch of sadness for the father she had never known and the grandfather they had left behind. "Mother said we left because she had no family. But you were here all along." Nancy looked up at him shyly.

Grandfather sighed, as if he was carrying a giant's weight on his shoulders. "Don't you go worrying yourself over the past. You and your mother have a happy life and that's all I ever wished for you both."

Nancy felt comforted by his words, but they didn't

answer the questions burning inside her. "But why did Mother and I leave here?" asked Nancy.

Grandfather's forehead crinkled. "It is a long and complicated tale, Nancy."

Nancy stood quietly, hoping that it was a tale he was prepared to tell.

From outside there was a sudden insistent banging on the shop door, like the beat of a drum.

Grandfather looked at the door in alarm. It was early and the shop was still closed, the blinds down, but Nancy could see the outline of a person behind the glass. Whoever was standing outside thumped on the door again.

Nancy watched the handle turn.

"I forgot to lock the door after my delivery boy left," said Nancy's grandfather, his eyes widening. "You mustn't be seen in here, Nancy. Quick, drop down behind the counter." Without any warning, he quickly took the pillow, stuffed it away and gently pushed Nancy to the floor where she crouched, her heart skipping.

The shop door opened and shut again, the bell emitting a loud jangle. Slow footsteps walked over to the counter. "Mr Greenstone. Good morning." It was a man's voice, and its steeliness sent a shiver across Nancy's shoulders.

"I will never bid *you* a good morning," replied her grandfather. His voice was cold as a tomb. Nancy's eyes were level with her grandfather's legs, and she saw him wipe his hands on his apron, then curl them into fists.

"Is that any way to greet your mayor?" replied the man coolly.

The mayor? There was a short pause, the silence filled with the ring of a bicycle bell, the bang of a motor-car exhaust backfiring.

"Why are you here *again*?" Nancy's grandfather asked the mayor tightly. "I need to ready the shop for opening."

Nancy jumped at the slap of two hands on the countertop. She sensed that the mayor was leaning towards her grandfather and thought she caught the minty smell of camphor toothpaste on his breath.

"And your shop is exactly the reason I have had to return, Mr Greenstone. I have been informed that the herbal tea you sold Mrs Bartholomew last week was infested with…mouse droppings." His words hung heavily in the air and her grandfather drew in a sharp breath.

Mouse droppings? But the shop was as clean as a new pin and her grandfather clearly took great pride in it.

"But Mrs Bartholomew has not shopped here for many years," Grandfather replied, his voice unsteady.

There was a sudden bump from upstairs. Nancy looked up at the ceiling. Was Violet jumping on the bed?

Nancy's grandfather coughed loudly.

"What was that noise?" asked the mayor.

"What noise?" replied Grandfather, his voice taut. He cast a nervous look up.

Nancy had a strong and sudden urge to offer some sort of support to her grandfather. But how could she while crouching on the floor trying to be invisible?

"Please. Won't you stop telling these lies about my shop and leave me be," said Grandfather, turning his attention back to the mayor.

The mayor laughed. "Never," he whispered with the force of a knife. "You took what was mine, so it is only right I continue to take from you."

Footsteps to the door. The jangle of the shop bell, the harsh slam of the door.

Nancy's grandfather let out an anguished cry and rushed round the counter. Nancy heard the click of

67

a key being inserted into the lock. "He is gone. You can get up now," he said.

Nancy stood up tentatively. The shop was just as before, but felt changed somehow, as if a cruel breeze had whipped through it, dimming the jars and bottles and polished countertop.

"The mayor…" Nancy started to say.

"He is as sour as vinegar," her grandfather interrupted, his face mottled pink.

"He was simply horrid to you!" exclaimed Nancy.

Nancy's grandfather shook his head. "I am sorry you overheard that," he said, his voice thick with emotion. "Please don't think badly of me. It is all untrue, Nancy. Every word that he said."

There was another bump from upstairs, the sound of voices. Violet and her mother.

Her grandfather looked to the ceiling and clasped his trembling hands together. "Oh dear, what will your mother say when she finds out you were in here when the mayor paid me one of his visits?"

Nancy remembered her mother's instruction to leave the shop before it opened. "Perhaps we needn't tell her?" she said haltingly, not wanting her grandfather to feel any worse than he did already.

Grandfather gave Nancy a grateful nod, walked behind the counter and pulled out the small pillow. He looked at it for a few seconds before pushing it into her hands and briefly clasping her fingers. "You are a good girl, Nancy. I am glad to have you here again." Her grandfather's eyes were hazy again, as if memories were clouding his vision.

Nancy thought about the mayor's allegation that her grandfather's tea was infested with mouse droppings. Telling such a lie would harm the reputation of the shop, could surely drive away customers. Her grandfather had said it was "one of the mayor's visits", which must mean he had come here and made these threats before. "What did the mayor mean when he said he'd continue to take from you? Did he mean…your customers?"

Nancy's grandfather nodded, pulled a handkerchief from his apron pocket and blew his nose loudly. He took off his spectacles and placed them on the counter, his shoulders suddenly bowed. He pressed the handkerchief to his lips and turned his back on Nancy.

Nancy's chin trembled at her grandfather's distress. "I'm sorry. I didn't mean to upset you." She glanced at the door to the house. "Shall I fetch Mother?"

Her grandfather shook his head, as he turned back to face her. "No. I just need a minute." He gave her a wobbly smile and smoothed the ends of his moustache. "Take the bag of provisions to the kitchen. There is bacon for breakfast."

Nancy picked up the bag, a little unsure whether she should leave him alone.

Her grandfather blew his nose again, stuffed the handkerchief into his pocket and looked at her. "Off you go, Nancy. I am fine, really. I shall make myself herbal tea. A teaspoon of chamomile and lemon balm and a pinch of ginger will set me right."

With the pillow in one hand and the bag of provisions in the other, Nancy left the shop and made her way downstairs to the kitchen. Her jaw tightened. If there was one thing she hated, it was people being treated unjustly. The mayor wanted to harm her grandfather's reputation and take away his customers. Why was the mayor treating her grandfather so unfairly, particularly when she was certain he had not done anything wrong? She needed to find answers to the questions building up in this strange house.

CHAPTER 9

Hide-and-seek

After a hearty breakfast of bacon, soft bread and creamy butter in the basement kitchen, Mother asked Nancy and Violet to fetch their aprons and help her clean the upper floors of the house. Nancy filled a pail of water at the kitchen sink, while looking up through the frosted glass of the basement window to the shadowy outline of the narrow back street above. The rattle of horses and carts, chatter of voices and thud of shoes on the cobbles clamoured in Nancy's head as she pondered over the mayor's visit to the shop.

The more she thought of it, the tighter the knot of

anger grew at the way her grandfather had been treated by that odious man. Nancy felt that on the whole she followed her parents' wishes and was obedient and well behaved, but she was not afraid to take action if she thought people were being treated unfairly. She had met her friend Josephine when she caught her cowering against the school railings one day, while Mildred Whipple tried to pilfer her new hair ribbons. Nancy had ended up scuffling with Mildred, who was in the year above and half a head taller, and they had both ended up in the headmistress's office for three raps of the dreaded cane across their palms as a result. Mildred had wept, but Nancy had swallowed back her tears, consoling herself with the thought that Josephine's ribbons had been saved.

Later, at home, Mother had bathed Nancy's sore palms, applied a herbal balm and said that while she was proud Nancy had stood up for Josephine, there were perhaps other ways she could have gone about it. "Millicent Garrett Fawcett is the leader of the national suffrage society and campaigns peacefully for reform but does not resort to violence to make herself heard. It is important to remember, Nancy, that words can be even more powerful than actions when fighting for change." Her mother's eyes had glistened as she spoke, and Nancy had vowed from then on to use her voice to seek change for the better whenever the need arose.

Carrying the sloshing pail of water upstairs, Nancy paused outside the internal door to the shop and listened. Her grandfather had opened up immediately after breakfast, but it was silent inside. No customers, just as her grandfather had predicted. She set to work washing down the dusty floorboards in her and Violet's bedroom, while Violet did forward rolls on the bed. "Aren't you going to help?" asked Nancy, sitting back on her heels, a spike of annoyance sitting in her chest.

"Cleaning is boring. I want to go out." Violet leaped from the bed, ran to the curtains which their mother had left half closed and yanked them fully open. Sunlight speared onto the damp floorboards. "Look what a lovely day it is outside!" She pulled on the curtains again and the brass rod they were attached to groaned. Nancy opened her mouth to tell Violet to stop pulling so hard, but she was too late. With a flurry of fallen plaster, one end of the curtain rod came away from the wall, the curtains sliding off into a forlorn heap on the floor.

"Oh," Violet said, her voice as limp as the curtains before her.

The sound of feet hurrying along the landing outside. Their mother bustled into the room, her apron streaked with dust. Her cheeks seemed even paler than earlier, her eyes even more hooded with tiredness. "Whatever has happened here?" she exclaimed, looking at the curtains. She glanced anxiously out of the window to the street below. A paperboy was standing on the street corner. "Comet news! Get your comet news here! Earthquake in Costa Rica blamed on arrival of Halley's comet!"

Violet was trying to lift the heavy curtains, her face pink with exertion. She dropped them at the cry of the paperboy. "An earthquake? Was it really caused by the comet?"

"Of course not," said their mother, her hands on her hips as she studied the fallen curtains. She looked up. "Violet, come away from the window!"

"I'm sorry, Mother," said Violet meekly, stepping back into the room. "I'm sorry for everything."

"You were supposed to be cleaning, helping your sister," said their mother with a frown.

Violet looked at Nancy sorrowfully and hung her head.

"She was helping," said Nancy quickly, realizing that

despite her annoyance at her little sister, she did not want her to get into any more trouble than she was already in. "It truly was an accident, Mother."

Violet looked up and flashed Nancy a thankful smile.

"I shall need your grandfather to fetch a stepladder to put these back up," said their mother. She pressed a hand to her forehead and sighed.

Nancy's insides constricted. Her mother looked unwell, exhausted in fact. "Why don't you go and rest? I'll play with Violet," she said.

Her mother dropped her chin. "Maybe I should have a lie-down. I did not sleep well last night and do feel so very tired. Just please…stay away from the windows." She gave Nancy a faint smile and her footsteps could be heard going up the stairs, as slow and heavy as if she was wading through mud.

"It really was an accident," Violet said in a small voice. "And I'm sorry I didn't help you with the cleaning."

"I know," said Nancy. "I just think we should try and do what Mother asks while we are here. She's tired and needs our help."

Violet looked to the door and the sound of their mother's retreating feet. "I miss Mother."

"What do you mean?" asked Nancy, sitting on the edge of her bed.

"She's…" Violet paused, rubbed her nose. "She's sadder in this house than at home. Like she's always thinking about something else, something secret."

Nancy looked at Violet's dejected face, realizing that her sister had put into words something she too had been thinking. "Yes. You're right," she said, admiring Violet's unexpected perceptiveness. She often ignored her little sister at home, feeling they had not much in common, and that was not just because Violet was five years younger. While Nancy liked sewing and quiet conversation, Violet liked riding her bicycle noisily down the street. While Nancy liked walking, Violet liked to skip. Where Nancy liked to consider her words, Violet mostly said what she was thinking. But here in this house it was just the two of them, living with a mother who had lost her old self and a grandfather they barely knew. She had an urge to cheer her sister up. "How about we do something fun? Like hide-and-seek? We haven't explored the rest of the house yet and I'm sure there are lots of places to hide," said Nancy.

Violet's face brightened and she nodded. "No cheating, though, you must count to one hundred."

"Don't I always?" said Nancy with a smile. "Go on then. Make sure you hide well, and please do be quiet, so we don't disturb Mother. And remember to keep away from the windows."

Violet grinned and slipped from the room, the creaks and groans of the floorboards echoing through the house as she went to find her hiding place.

Nancy lay back on her bed and counted slowly. Her eyes traced the cracks in the ceiling, her thoughts connecting them like a dot-to-dot picture.

1, 2, 3… Why had their mother lied about having no remaining family and kept their grandfather a secret all these years?

23, 24, 25… Their grandfather did not appear to be ill, so why had they come to stay?

55, 56, 57… The more Nancy thought of it, the more peculiar the instructions to stay inside the house and away from the windows seemed.

62, 63, 64… Was the reason for their visit something to do with the messages she had heard her mother mention early that morning?

87, 88, 89… Their grandfather seemed like a nice and honest man. Why would the mayor of this town make up such horrid lies about him and drive his customers away?

On the count of one hundred, Nancy pushed her thoughts to one side, walked past the crumpled curtains and out onto the landing where she stood listening. It was so quiet, it almost seemed as if the fragrant herbs and bottles and jars of oil were holding their breath and listening with her.

She started her hunt for Violet in a room at the back of the house, discovering a drawing room decorated in a cacophony of colours: striped green-and-cream flowered wallpaper, sumptuous red velvet curtains edged with gold fringing and a large orange and blue rug. The heavy furniture was hidden under dust sheets, but there was no Violet.

Her grandfather appeared to spend most of his time in the small wood-panelled library next to the drawing room, where the smell of pipe smoke hovered in the air and crumbs dusted a small console table next to a threadbare, but comfortable, easy chair. In the bedroom next door to the library she found an enormous mahogany bed and matching wardrobe, but Violet was not hiding under or inside either of those objects. Where could she be?

Her favourite places to hide at home were on window ledges behind curtains or inside their parents' wardrobe, behind Father's suits and shirts. A pang of longing for her father and their home in Leeds momentarily winded Nancy and she folded her arms round her middle and waited for the ache to pass. Nancy looked down the stairwell to the ground floor. All was quiet down there too, still no sound of any customers in the shop. She tipped her head upwards, thought she could hear voices from the floor above and the sound of a door creaking shut. Perhaps Violet had come across Mother while trying to find a hiding place?

She crept up to the second floor, glancing at their mother's closed bedroom door. Her grandfather's door was closed too, and Nancy was sure her sister would not have dared to hide in there. Nancy looked up the staircase leading to the attic rooms, light from the stairwell grazing the polished wooden bannister and strange gargoyles. Would Violet have gone to the top of the house? Maybe, for she had been quite taken with the embroidered pillowslip and Nancy's tale of the discovery of the room she had slept in as a baby.

Nancy ran lightly up the stairs. A faint tapping noise came from above her head. She frowned, looked up at the final narrow set of stairs leading to the cupola. Grandfather had made it clear visiting the cupola was forbidden. She scrunched her nose, suddenly remembering that Violet hadn't been with her when he had issued that instruction, and she had not thought to tell her sister. She did not want to disobey her grandfather, but intrigue carried her up the stairs and she stooped to avoid hitting her head on the low ceiling. The light grew brighter the higher she climbed and then, all of a sudden, she found herself at the top of the house.

CHAPTER 10

The Cupola

Nancy's eyes widened in surprise as she looked around the cupola at the top of the house. She felt as if she was standing in the lamp room of a miniature lighthouse. Sun streamed through the four arched windows, throwing rainbow beads of light around the white walls of the small octagonal room. It was only large enough for perhaps four people – and that would be a squeeze. Two enclosed wooden benches with midnight-blue velvet cushions ran along two sides of the octagon, and in the centre of the room stood a tall brass telescope, its glass eye pointing out of a window to her left.

She whirled round on the spot.

The view from up here was quite tremendous; it had to be the highest point in the whole town. Nancy could see the green of the countryside, the tiny dark dots of animals in the fields. She could see town rooftops, a patchwork of different-coloured roof slates, twisting chimneys and bricks. She could see the street below and the boy selling newspapers she had heard from her room earlier on.

It was like being a bird in the sky, looking down on the world from a secret tower. And if this is what it was like in the daytime, just imagine what it would be like at night! The cupola gave the old house a magnificence that made Nancy fully appreciate her grandfather's pride at it being kept in their family for so many years.

A *tap-tap-tap* from under one of the benches echoed around the small space. Nancy wobbled and reached out a hand to steady herself, almost knocking the telescope off its stand. The blue seat-cushion to her right was rocking from side to side like a boat. What was happening? Then she remembered why she had come up here. "Violet? Is that you?" Nancy whispered.

"Yes," squeaked a muffled voice from inside the

bench. "I rather think the cushion's got stuck. Can you help?"

Nancy tugged at the end of the cushion, prising it free along with her little sister, who uncurled from her hiding place like a woodlouse.

"You took ages," Violet said, standing up and stretching, her cheeks flushed. "It wasn't my first hiding place, but this one is a lot better. Isn't this room smashing? We could play up here, have tea parties…"

Nancy noticed then that Violet had something in her hand. "What's that?" she asked, helping her sister climb out of the bench.

"I found it in here." The small blue book with gold lettering had a picture of children looking up at the night sky on the cover. *Easy Guide to the Constellations*.

Nancy took it from her sister and flicked through it. There were pictures inside of the constellations and a pencil-scrawled name on the inside cover. *Mr Percival Douglas*.

Violet pressed her nose to one of the arched windows. "Look, do you see the cows, Nancy? We're so close to the countryside. And see that big building with the high wall over there? What do you think that is? And what about this marvellous telescope? Do you think we would be allowed up here to watch the comet? What does this little wheel on the telescope do? Oh, Nancy. Help!"

THUMP!

Nancy dropped the astronomy book back inside the bench Violet had been hiding in and swallowed a gasp as she saw what had happened. The telescope had slipped to one side, its fall broken by the bench.

"Violet, what have you done!" Nancy cried, rushing to right the telescope. It was heavier than it looked, and she struggled to lift it. Grandfather had said this was an antique, which meant it must be valuable. She sorely hoped it was not broken.

Footsteps thundered up the twisting stairs. "Girls?" Their mother, white-faced with alarm. There was little room for her in the cupola. They were like three giants trying to fit inside a shoe. "What in heaven's name!" she exclaimed, looking at the fallen telescope.

"I'm sorry, Mother," said Violet in a glum voice. "I'm really, truly ever so sorry."

Their mother's lips pressed together as she helped Nancy right the telescope. She pointed it towards the same window it had been looking out of before and glanced through the eyepiece. "It is out of focus, but luckily does not seem to be broken. I thought your grandfather had told you not to come up here?" Her look was withering and made Nancy feel as small as a pea.

"I don't think Violet knew that. We were only playing hide-and-seek," she said.

"I asked you to look after Violet and stay hidden, but in the space of a morning we've had a broken curtain rod and a fallen telescope. This will not do," said their mother, exasperation pulling her voice as tight as a knot.

"They honestly were accidents. It's difficult having to stay inside," said Nancy, wondering again at Mother's insistence they keep hidden, but also sensing she would not take kindly to being questioned about this now.

"Oh, it is dull! Can't we please go out? It's boring in the house," said Violet. "On Saturdays at home Father takes us to the park with Monty."

Mother simply shook her head and gestured for the girls to go ahead of her down the stairs as she turned to replace the velvet bench-cushion.

Nancy glanced back at her mother, who reached inside the bench, picked up the book on the constellations then dropped it like a hot coal. But that wasn't the only thing Nancy noticed. The telescope was not tilted to the sky, but was level with the rooftops of the town. She was certain it had been like that when she entered the cupola too, which meant that her mother and grandfather might not have been looking at the comet last night, but something else entirely. Her fingers itched to curl round the barrel of the telescope so she could peer through the viewfinder and discover what it was pointing at. As she walked down the stairs this disobedient urge began to grow, and she wondered when she might be able to return to the cupola to see what she could find out.

CHAPTER 11

Package

After Grandfather had fixed the rod and refitted the curtains in their bedroom, which Mother insisted were kept partly drawn, Nancy and Violet were instructed to sit on their beds with their needlework and not to move an inch for the remainder of the day.

Violet was sullen as she clumsily stitched red ribbon to the edge of the handkerchief she was working on in the dim light. "Why must we always be making boring handkerchiefs for the suffragists?" she asked glumly.

"They are for a worthy and important cause, Violet," said Nancy, working on her own handkerchief slowly and steadily, the motion of binding the ribbon to the cloth soothing her. Violet might not find sewing absorbing, but Nancy did, often sitting beside their parents in the evenings as she quietly threaded, snipped and stitched, listening to them speak about their days.

"You need to accept that all girls must be proficient in needlework," said their mother, on the frequent occasions when Violet planted her feet on the floor and refused to sew another stitch.

"But why?" Violet would moan dramatically.

"When you run your own household, clothing will always need mending. And see how your handkerchiefs are helping the suffragist movement," Mother would reply, as Father looked on, the corners of his lips upturned in amusement at Violet's protestations.

What was their father doing now? Nancy missed his quiet conversation, his tales of the people he was defending in court. She was proud of the fact his solicitor's practice defended those most in need, often taking a reduced payment if it was a case they were particularly passionate about. "Sometimes people end up on the wrong side of the law because of poor judgement and it is important to help them turn their lives around," he would say, telling them a tale of a woman who ended up in Leeds Gaol for organizing a protest march to support the suffrage movement. She had been sent to prison for six weeks and upon her release a kite was flown over the prison bearing the words "Votes for Women".

Mother would often lean forward, her eyes glistening and eager when he spoke of such matters, and Nancy sometimes wondered if she was envious of Father's career in law. But when Nancy had once asked her father if there was a chance *she* might one day follow in his footsteps, he had shaken his head and frowned. "Women are not yet permitted to practise law, Nancy. I hope that one day this may change, but in the meantime work hard at your lessons and uphold your good morals. They will get you far."

That night, after eating a very subdued supper and being sent to bed early, Nancy awoke in the dark to the ten o'clock chimes on the landing and the sound of groaning floorboards and conversations that once again were too distant to hear properly.

A blade of moonlight coming through a gap in the curtains lit a path to the door. Nancy sprang out of bed and crept to it, wincing as it creaked open, but thankfully Violet slept on. Tonight she did not have to go as far as the cupola to hear what was being said, for the stairs creaked again and her mother appeared wearing a long, dark cloak, the hood pulled up around her tired, pale face. Her grandfather was close behind carrying a flickering oil lamp in one hand, and a small, flat package wrapped in brown paper in the other. "Here," he said, passing her mother the package, which she immediately pushed into her cloak pocket.

"Thank you," said her mother in a tight voice.

"You are happy to take the message alone, Charlotte?" asked her grandfather, his voice high and anxious.

"Yes. Don't worry, I shall keep to the shadows. It's best you stay in case the children awaken," her mother replied.

"Please be careful," said Grandfather, embracing her quickly. "I shall go up to the cupola and watch."

Nancy drew in a whisper-quiet breath as she stood behind the door and thought again of the telescope pointing across the town.

"I am sorry the girls disobeyed you and went up there," said Mother.

"They were just curious, no harm was done," he said softly.

"But they must not discover what we are doing," said Mother.

Grandfather gave a quick nod of agreement.

Mother took the oil lamp from Grandfather and walked swiftly down the stairs. There was the distant thud of the door closing in the basement kitchen. Where was her mother going?

Nancy shut her bedroom door carefully and crept back into bed, wishing with all her might she could go up to the cupola and see what her grandfather was looking at through the telescope. She listened to the sound of Violet breathing, watched a sliver of moonlight creep across the floorboards, heard the clock on the landing chime eleven o'clock, all the while wondering who the package was intended for, and what secrets Mother was keeping.

A short while after that Nancy heard the thump of the back door and the sound of her mother's footsteps climbing the stairs to bed. She rolled over, her eyes aching with tiredness, resolving that one way or another she would get answers to her questions.

The next morning began in a similar manner to the previous one, with Nancy helping her grandfather in the closed shop, except this time there was no unexpected visit from the mayor. Nancy polished the glass cabinets and the countertop, but there were no other tasks for her, no stock to replenish or herb drawers to refill. "Did you and Mother watch the comet through your telescope last night?" she asked, smothering a yawn as she folded the cloth and placed the tin of beeswax polish in the store cupboard.

"Yes," said her grandfather glumly, opening the cash register and staring at the empty drawers.

"Did you watch it for a long time?" asked Nancy, hoping he might drop a hint as to what he was really doing in the cupola, for she was sure he was not watching the comet.

Grandfather gave her a quick glance. "Yes. It was the brightest I've ever seen it." His face was as glum as his voice, and she knew he was lying. Last night the moon was bright, which would have made the comet more difficult to see. Nancy was about to question him further, without giving away what she knew, when there was a cry from above, followed by the clattering of feet down the stairs. Nancy and her grandfather exchanged a look of alarm.

Nancy's mother flew into the shop, her hand gripping Violet's wrist. "I am at my wits' end," she cried, shaking her head. Her hair was loose, and she was still in her nightdress. Nancy swallowed back her unease. Her mother did not behave like this at home. She was always up and dressed with breakfast on the table by the time they came downstairs in the morning.

"What has happened?" asked Grandfather, his brow creasing.

"Violet has knocked over one of the jars of lavender oil on the first-floor landing," said Mother, loosening Violet's wrist before pressing her own fingers to her temples.

"I was just having a look," said Violet, brushing a tear from her cheek. "I'm sorry, Mother. I'm sorry, Grandfather. I'll clean it up."

"I just…wish you could be still for five minutes," sighed their mother, her voice softening.

"They need to go out," said their grandfather, folding his arms. "It is no good them being cooped up in here with us."

Nancy looked at Grandfather with surprise.

"But they must stay in. That is what we decided," said their mother.

"Well it seems we made the wrong decision. It's not right keeping them in the house. If no one sees them leave and they walk down Abbeygate Street to the Botanic Gardens and back, what harm can befall them? Especially if they don't talk to anyone," said their grandfather.

Mother looked uncertain. "You mean let them go out on their own?"

Their grandfather gave a small shrug. "Well, we cannot go with them."

"Why not?" asked Nancy.

"We just can't," said their mother, fiddling with the buttons at the neck of her nightdress.

Nancy frowned, thinking back to her mother's errand the night before. Why on earth could they not leave the house together?

"Let them go, Charlotte," their grandfather urged again.

A bubble of hope rose within Nancy. It was so hard to keep Violet out of trouble and occupied indoors and she felt as cooped up as a moth in a jar. "Father says that even prisoners are allowed time outside. And it is Sunday. Shouldn't we be going to church, Mother?" she said, hoping this might persuade her.

Their mother's fingers dropped from her temples and she threw what seemed to be a despairing look at Grandfather, before turning her gaze back to Nancy. "There will be no church while we are staying here."

"What harm will it do to let them go out?" said Grandfather softly, placing a hand on their mother's right arm. "The shops are shut and town is quiet on a Sunday."

Mother blinked and Nancy was suddenly afraid that she was going to cry. "Very well," she said limply. "You may go out after breakfast. But you must do as your grandfather says. Leave by the basement door, wear your aprons and hats, keep your heads down and speak to no one. Go directly to the Botanic Gardens and back again." She rubbed the nape of her neck, her look at Nancy piercing. "I am trusting you to follow my instructions, Nancy. Do you understand?"

"Yes, Mother," said Nancy, glancing at Violet, who was already hopping up and down with excitement. She also felt a rising excitement at getting out of this odd house. It might provide the opportunity to get answers to some of her questions and discover why their mother was behaving so strangely, wanting to keep them hidden away inside.

CHAPTER 12

The Fall

Sunshine reflected off the pastel-painted buildings. Families walked to church in their Sunday best, girls dressed in ankle-length white dresses and straw boaters, boys in jackets, waistcoats and caps. Following Grandfather's directions to the top of Abbeygate Street, Nancy could see wooded hills and the countryside, so close that she felt she could taste the ripeness of spring in the air. It was so different to the air in Leeds, thick with factory smuts and exhaust fumes from cars and omnibuses, and it made her feel a little lost and overwhelmed.

Violet grinned and hopped by her side like a bird released from its cage. "Look at that," she exclaimed, pointing at two men balancing precariously on the tops of ladders attaching a midnight-blue banner across the entrance to the street. The edges of the banner were decorated with images of silvery comets, long tails bursting out behind them.

Beyond the banner, Nancy saw that many shops down the hilly street had put up their own brightly coloured flags and bunting. Violet skipped past the pretty shopfronts, so different from Leeds city centre's tall gothic buildings, turrets and spires. Nancy began to follow her sister, but paused when her eyes were drawn to a poster in the window of a wine merchant's shop, where a man with a very red nose was pressing soft putty into the gaps around the door frame.

Comet Party!

The mayor invites you to celebrate
the earth passing through the tail of Halley's comet

on Wednesday 18th May at the
Subscription Rooms.

Viewing telescopes and field glasses provided!

Ladies to dress in the colours of the sky.

All ticket proceeds to charity.

"A comet party," Nancy murmured, feeling a tingle of excitement. She'd read in her father's newspaper of fashionable comet parties taking place in many countries across the globe on the night the comet was closest to Earth, now only three days away.

The festivities were to last all night long, with boat trips on the River Seine in Paris and people dancing on hotel rooftops in New York. These were people who embraced the arrival of the comet and were excited by it, seeing it as an extraordinary event to be celebrated. Nancy wished she could tell her friend Josephine about the party. A few weeks ago, Josephine had bravely put her hand up in class, asking the teacher if they could have a school celebration to mark the comet's arrival. Their teacher had frowned, said absolutely not and that Josephine should concentrate her efforts on improving her playing of the piano rather than thinking about celestial objects in the sky. Nancy had felt Josephine's disappointment keenly, having imagined the fun of this party herself.

Nancy looked again at Violet, who had skipped onwards. Violet glanced back and waved and Nancy held up a hand, signalling her sister to stop.

"What are you doing there, Mr Thompson?"

Nancy turned and saw a man, in a navy-blue apron carrying a tray of shiny red lobsters, pause in front of the man working putty into his door frame.

"I thought I should seal up the gaps in my door just in case those scientists are right, and the comet gas can seep through nooks and crannies," said Mr Thompson.

The man with the lobsters grimaced. "These dire reports of the comet are not made by scientists, but by sensation makers. Don't believe all that you read."

"It's unusual to see you working on a Sunday. Are you preparing for the mayor's party?" Mr Thompson asked, looking around as if anxious of being overheard. He noticed Nancy watching and frowned.

Nancy stared again at the poster, her ears warm with guilt at listening in, but eager to hear what they were saying about the mayor.

"Of course," said the lobster-carrying man. "Just like the rest of this town."

"Are those lobsters for the mayor?" asked Mr Thompson.

"Yes. Only the finest will do," said the man, but his voice was as bitter as squeezed lemons.

"I'm supplying only the finest and most expensive wines for the party too," replied Mr Thompson. His voice was also sour. Nancy frowned. These men didn't seem very pleased about supplying the mayor with fine food and drink. In fact, they seemed to dislike him.

With a lurch, Nancy realized she had forgotten about Violet. Her sister had ignored the instruction to stop and had skipped halfway down the hill. Leaving the men to their conversation, Nancy walked swiftly on, past Olivers and Sons Grocers, where the smell of fresh coffee and laughter spilled out from an upstairs window; past Thurlow Champness Jeweller; past F. W. Groom Bookseller, where a man was hanging silver cardboard stars around a display of astronomy charts in his window; past Cavendish's Haberdashery where a woman was cleaning the shop windows with a cloth and pail of soapy water. The shops might be closed, but there was a sense of bustle and activity as people readied themselves for a new working week and the mayor's party.

"Slow down, Violet," Nancy called, as she neared the end of the street and a large stone gateway, which Grandfather had said marked the entrance to the Botanic Gardens. But Violet did not hear, or perhaps she chose not to hear, preferring instead to stretch her legs and skip like the wind, not caring that her straw hat had tilted to one side, her plaits were loosening and her socks had fallen to her ankles.

"Violet," exclaimed Nancy again, drawing a curious and disapproving look from a man and woman dressed in Sunday-best black.

"You might expect that behaviour from a boy, but from a girl! On a Sunday as well," she heard the woman exclaim in disgust.

Nancy's jaw tightened. Mother was trusting her to ensure that there were no mishaps on the trip to the gardens and she was determined there wouldn't be.

There was a crossroads near the end of the street and Nancy saw the shiny black motor car approaching the junction, but Violet hadn't. Her head was tilted to the flags and banners as she skipped. The scene seemed to unfold before Nancy in slow motion. The shout of the man in the car as he saw her sister. The screech of the wheels on the dusty road. The blood-curdling cry from Violet who skidded to the ground with a whump, her straw hat breaking free from its ribbons and rolling off down the hill like a small wheel.

Nancy raced to her sister on jelly-like legs. *Please be all right, Violet, please be all right,* she screamed inside her head.

"I didn't see her. She came from nowhere," cried the man, climbing out of the car and removing his driving goggles.

Violet was lying flat on her back breathing heavily, her eyes closed.

"Talk to me, Violet. Are you hurt?" pleaded Nancy, kneeling beside her sister, her heart thudding too fast in her chest.

The couple in black, who had seconds ago been admonishing her and Violet's behaviour, rushed over, asking if they could do anything to help.

Violet's eyes flicked open, tears springing to them. "Ow, my elbow. It's sore, Nancy."

A boy kneeled next to Nancy. She turned and looked at him. It was the tall, spindly boy who had delivered her grandfather's provisions the day before. Today he was dressed in brown tweed trousers and a waistcoat, the sleeves of his cream shirt rolled to the elbows.

He peered anxiously at Violet, who was now trying to sit up. "I saw what happened from the haberdashery shop. I came to see if I could help."

"Careful. She may have broken a bone," said the woman in black, who had pulled out her lace handkerchief and was dabbing her nose daintily, as if the whole event was too much for her nerves.

"I don't think anything's broken," said Violet shakily.

"Can you wiggle your toes, and your fingers? That's it. I think you will live," said the black-suited man, returning Violet's runaway hat to Nancy.

Nancy sat back on her heels in relief, clutching the hat to her chest.

The driver of the car let out a long sigh at the realization that Violet would recover. "Where are your parents, are they nearby?" he said, wringing his hands together.

"We were sent out for a walk on our own," Nancy replied, noticing with a sickening lurch that the right sleeve of her sister's dress was ripped and blood was seeping into the white muslin from a nasty gash on her elbow. Nancy placed the hat down, pulled out her handkerchief and held it to the wound, wishing that

Mother was there with one of her remedies. Violet's cheeks scrunched in pain.

"My ma's just up the street in our shop. She'll have you patched up in no time," said the boy, helping Violet to her feet. "I'm Burch, by the way. From your conversation just now I'm guessing you're Nancy, and this is Violet? I've seen you before, haven't I, Nancy?"

Nancy nodded, then remembered with a pinch their mother's strict instruction not to talk to strangers and hung her head. Not only had Violet got injured, now this boy knew their names. What was supposed to be a quick outing to the Botanic Gardens had instead taken a terrible turn and she'd let her mother down in the worst possible way.

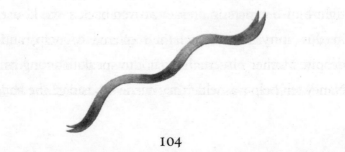

CHAPTER 13

Humiliation

Nancy felt a little sick as she looked at the crimson stain spreading onto the handkerchief that Violet was pressing gingerly to her elbow. After she had reassured the driver of the car that he was not to blame and that her sister would recover, Nancy and Burch helped Violet walk slowly back up the street towards the haberdashery shop. Nancy imagined their mother's tight-lipped expression if they arrived back at the house in this sorry state. Burch had offered to help, and despite Mother's instructions not to speak to strangers, Nancy felt help was what they needed; besides, she had seen Burch talking to her grandfather in the apothecary shop, so he wasn't a true stranger.

"I saw you at Mr Greenstone's yesterday," said Burch after a few steps. "I've never known him to have visitors."

"Oh…um…he hasn't been well," said Nancy. "Mother, Violet and I have come to help him watch the comet." The words popped out by accident and she felt a sliver of regret. But with Burch's offer of help it would be churlish to say nothing. Perhaps she could keep the conversation to the bare facts. Nancy paused and adjusted her grip on Violet's hand. "We were on our way to the Botanic Gardens, but we weren't supposed to talk to strangers," she said. "I was to look after my sister and now it's all gone dreadfully wrong."

"Not quite the outing you planned," said Burch sympathetically. He looked ahead and Nancy saw the woman who had been cleaning the windows of the haberdashery earlier on. She was standing on the step of the shop watching them with concern. "That's my ma. But, I must tell you, she doesn't know I make deliveries to Greenstone's," said Burch.

"Oh," said Nancy. "Why not?"

"If you're staying with Mr Greenstone, I suppose you

already know he's got a poor reputation around here," said Burch, giving her a sidelong glance.

"Oh," said Nancy, thinking about the mayor's visit to her grandfather's shop the day before and the harsh words he had thrown at Grandfather.

"But Mr Greenstone's always been good to me, paid my wages and treated me well," said Burch. "I like him."

"Mr Greenstone's our grandfather," said Violet in a small voice.

Nancy looked at her sister with dismay. In the space of a few minutes Burch had learned more about them than their mother would have approved of. Mother had wanted to keep them inside, but what *were* the risks of her and Violet being seen in this town?

"You're Mr Greenstone's granddaughters?" Burch said, his eyes widening.

"We didn't know he was our grandfather until two days ago," said Violet, poking her elbow with a finger and wincing as they continued towards the shop.

"Is that right?" said Burch, giving Nancy another glance, as if he had questions he would very much like to ask.

Nancy suddenly wondered whether she should take Violet directly back to the house to avoid any further questioning. But it was too late; the woman who had been cleaning the windows of the haberdashery was almost upon them, giving them a wide and concerned smile.

"Oh dear, what an accident you have had," she said, looking at Violet's elbow and ushering them into the shop. Burch's mother was as tall and thin as her son, with wide eyes that exuded the warmth of a summer's day. She sat Violet on the countertop and gave her a clothing catalogue to look at, while bustling away to fetch some warm water and gauze to clean her wound.

Nancy took in the contents of the shop; the collection of shimmering fabrics on the back wall, a floor-to-ceiling cabinet of small drawers with examples of the objects inside stuck to the front – thimbles, different-sized scissors, pliers, crochet hooks, knitting needles and buttons organized by size, shape and colour. The effect was bright and busy and gave the shop a homely feel.

"You're very tall," Violet said to Burch, who was standing against the counter watching them.

"Violet," said Nancy, hoping her sister's words had not caused offence.

But a slow grin was spreading across Burch's face.

His reedy cheeks puffed up and a bellow of bell-like laughter burst from his lips. Nancy blinked in surprise. His laugh sounded out of place, like it should belong to someone half his height and twice his width, and it made her smile. Even Violet seemed to forget her sore elbow and managed a small grin.

"At least my name matches my height. My grandpa worked in a timber yard and had a fondness for trees – my ma's called Hazel. I was named after the birch tree but my folks changed it a little to make it more of a name. It could have been worse, I suppose, they could have called me Oak or Yew."

"Or Horse Chestnut," said Violet with a giggle.

Burch grinned again. "So how long are you staying in town for?"

"Mother said until the comet starts to fade, which is after Wednesday, I suppose," said Nancy.

"After the comet party then," said Burch, his eyebrows pulling together as if he was not looking forward to it.

"I saw a poster about the party near the wine merchant's shop," said Nancy.

"Is that why there are flags and decorations everywhere?" asked Violet.

Burch nodded. "It's all the town's spoken of for months. The mayor's made sure of that." A shadow crossed his face which Nancy did not understand, for she felt quite envious of those attending such a celebration.

"It's the mayor's party then?" asked Nancy with interest.

Burch nodded again. "He has a few grand parties every year to raise money for charitable causes, but this is to be the biggest one yet. It's at the Subscription Rooms. I'm not much looking forward to it though."

"What are the Subscription Rooms?" asked Nancy.

"It's the name of a building near here on Angel Hill, used for social gatherings," he replied.

"Are you talking of the comet party?" asked Burch's mother, returning with a small bowl of warm water and gauze. She carefully removed the handkerchief that Nancy had wound round Violet's grazed elbow and placed it on the counter. "Burch's pa has worked such long hours helping the mayor prepare for the celebration," she said, dabbing at Violet's skin.

"It's meant more work for us in the shop," said Burch.

"Oh," said Nancy, thinking that could be the reason he wasn't very enthusiastic about the party.

"My Philip drives the mayor around in his fancy red motor car too," said Burch's mother with a sniff, as if she did not approve. "He has to wear a chauffeur's hat that makes his head look as thin as a pin."

There was a cough from outside the open shop door and Burch's mother turned. "Oh, Mayor Douglas. We were just…speaking of you." Her cheeks reddened.

A man about the same age as Nancy's father with skin as pale as a pearl entered the shop. A pocket watch dangled on a gold chain from his smartly tailored jacket. He took off his black hat and smoothed his silky-brown hair. His upright posture and well-cut clothes suggested an air of wealth and importance, someone to be listened to. He was handsome and did not fit the musty image of a mayor with greying hair and curling sideburns that Nancy had imagined, while cowering behind the apothecary shop counter, the day before. She shrank to the back of the shop and stood by Violet, thought again of the words the mayor had thrown at her grandfather.

The mayor's eyes narrowed and fixed on Burch's mother. "Good day, Mrs Cavendish. Where is your husband this morning?" he asked, his tone direct and forthright.

"Oh…I…um. It's Sunday, Mayor. He doesn't work

on a Sunday," said Mrs Cavendish. She tilted her lips into a smile which didn't reach her eyes.

The mayor gave Mrs Cavendish a withering look. "Well, he is working today."

Nancy saw Burch shift on his feet, a muscle twitching his jaw.

"Burch," said the mayor, his voice as silky as one of the fabrics on the back wall of the shop.

"Yes?" said Burch, staring the mayor right in the eye.

The mayor's eyes narrowed. "Don't you mean, 'Yes, Mayor'?"

There was a short pause and Mrs Cavendish cleared her throat.

"Yes, Mayor," said Burch, his hands slowly balling into fists.

"Fetch your father," said the mayor, glancing at his pocket watch and tapping it. "Now!"

Burch's mouth slackened as he looked to his mother then back to the mayor.

"Burch. Please go and see if your pa is upstairs," pleaded Mrs Cavendish in a low voice.

"But it's Sunday. Pa hasn't had a day off in months," Burch replied in an equally low voice.

The mayor took a step towards Burch.

Nancy stood closer to Violet, the hairs on her arms prickling at the mayor's cold demeanour.

Burch's cheeks turned puce, as if the mayor had gripped him in his fist and squeezed. Without saying another word, Burch turned on his heel and headed to the back of the shop and through a door. Thumps could be heard on the stairs, then the hum of raised voices from above.

Nancy felt a clench of sympathy. The mayor had a horrid way of speaking to people besides her grandfather and she wondered if he treated all acquaintances like this. She stepped even closer to Violet, who was still absorbed in the clothing catalogue, hoping that the mayor would not turn his attention to them. Should they leave? The atmosphere in the shop was heavy with the weight of something she didn't understand.

Burch returned quickly, followed by a man with hooded eyes and a frame as stooped as a branch that had bent in a storm and not been able to right itself. He snapped his braces into place and pulled on his grey jacket. "Mayor. I thought we agreed that you didn't require my services today," said Burch's father reverently. His head bobbed and for a second Nancy wondered if he was bowing.

A stiff smile skirted the mayor's lips. "My shoes need shining before I go to church."

Mrs Cavendish drew in a breath and pressed a hand to her neck.

Burch rubbed an eyelid, his lips set in a hard line.

Burch's father quickly did up the buttons on his jacket and smoothed the creases from his sleeves. "Of course. And where are the shoes that need shining?"

The mayor looked down at his gleaming black, leather shoes. "On. My. Feet." He said each word slowly and deliberately, staring Burch's father right in the eye.

Nancy stifled a gasp. The mayor expected Burch's father to get down on his hands and knees and clean his shoes now, right here in the shop? But that was outrageous, and her cheeks burned at the thought. She remembered an occasion when Josephine had been called up to the teacher's desk at school after she had failed to fully memorize her French verbs. The teacher had made her stand in front of the class for the remainder of the lesson, her French book balanced on her head. Nancy's father had been furious when she had told him what happened. "Humiliation is one of the worst forms of bullying," he'd said angrily. "Its only purpose is to make a person feel small and inferior."

Burch's father remained impassive to his own humiliation, showing not a hint of emotion as he considered the mayor's instruction. Pulling a neatly folded handkerchief from his pocket, he bent down and began to rub the mayor's already-shiny shoes.

The mayor watched him; his chest puffed out like a cockerel.

Mrs Cavendish turned away and fiddled with the collar on her blouse.

Burch's eyebrows tugged together, and he glanced at Nancy and Violet worriedly.

Nancy felt a little light-headed as she watched, wondering what caused the mayor to behave in this terrible way.

As Mr Cavendish busied himself shining the mayor's shoes, Mrs Cavendish busied herself tending to Violet's elbow. Nancy and Burch stood to the rear of the shop in silence, Nancy's insides burning in indignation at the sight of Mr Cavendish on his knees before the mayor. The mayor's shoes had already been gleaming when he had walked into the shop and Nancy could not fathom why he could not clean them himself, especially as it was Burch's father's day off.

"Thank you, Cavendish. You may stop now," said the mayor a short while later. "You need to go to the observatory in the Subscription Rooms and continue with the comet party preparations. There are telescopes and field glasses to be polished. And tomorrow you must finish collecting the ticket money from people who have not yet paid. This is all for charity. Remember that." He looked down at his mirror-like shoes with a smug satisfaction.

Mr Cavendish didn't look at his wife or son, merely nodded, stood up and jammed his cap on his head and shuffled from the shop.

Nancy looked to Violet, whose elbow had been bound with gauze. They needed to leave. She tapped her sister on the leg, beckoned for her to get down from the counter, but saw with alarm that the mayor was walking deeper into the shop towards the very spot where they were standing.

CHAPTER 14

Trust

Nancy kept her head low as the mayor strode towards them at the rear of the haberdashery shop. "Will you be making any deliveries to the chemist shops on Monday or Tuesday? Perhaps Croasdale's…or even Greenstone's?" he asked Burch. The last word was stated in the way you might address a sworn enemy you were about to face in a duel.

Nancy lifted her chin a little at the mention of her grandfather's shop.

"I'm afraid not, Mayor," said Burch steadily. "As you know, Ma doesn't permit me to deliver to Greenstone's."

The mayor's jaw twitched, and his eyes darkened. "Of course. Quite right too. It would be ill-judged for *anyone* in this town to associate with Mr Greenstone."

"Why?"

Nancy wondered why the mayor, Mrs Cavendish and Burch were all suddenly staring at her, then she realized with a start that rather than saying the word silently in her head, she'd said it out loud. A wave of heat engulfed her.

The mayor looked at Nancy, his eyes straying to Violet sitting on the counter. He frowned. "Are these friends of yours, Burch?" He looked at them a bit harder. "Might we be introduced?"

"Um. They're just about to leave," said Burch quickly.

Nancy caught Burch's eye and he seemed to be trying to convey something to her silently.

The mayor peered at Nancy, blinked.

Nancy swallowed. She hoped that Violet would continue looking at the clothing catalogue and stay quiet.

"I. Said. Might. We. Be. Introduced." The mayor's words were precise and as clear as a whistle and said with such force and intent that Nancy felt he would persist until he got an answer.

Mrs Cavendish gave Nancy an encouraging smile. "Go on, dear. Don't be shy."

Nancy's mouth felt as parched as a desert. She swallowed again.

The mayor continued to stare at Nancy. His alabaster cheeks were becoming mottled and he suddenly coughed. He coughed again and pressed a hand to his lips.

Mrs Cavendish flapped around him like a mother hen. "Oh…are you unwell…? Shall I fetch a glass of water, Mayor?"

The mayor seemed to be struggling to catch his breath and he gave Mrs Cavendish a sharp nod.

Nancy stood there helplessly. Was the mayor about to keel over in the haberdashery shop? He coughed some more then turned back to face Nancy. "I believe a…mackerel bone is lodged in my throat from breakfast," he said weakly. He took the glass of water Mrs Cavendish had hurried back with and swallowed it down in one big gulp, all the while looking at Nancy from the corner of his eye.

Passing Mrs Cavendish the empty glass, he approached the shop counter and Violet in cautious steps, his eyes sweeping to her bound elbow. To Nancy's surprise, the mayor picked up the bloodstained handkerchief Nancy had used to bind Violet's wound between two fingers, holding it in front of him as if it were a dead rat. "Most unsanitary to leave items like this lying around. Who does it belong to?"

"Um, it's mine," Nancy said. The mayor offered her the handkerchief and she took it from him, stuffing it into her apron pocket.

"Did you sew the edging for the handkerchief? You are good at needlework," chattered Mrs Cavendish, who seemed desperate to ease the knife-like tension simmering in the air.

The mayor suddenly turned to the door. "I have a busy day ahead of me," he murmured. He put his hat back on and tipped it. "Good day to you all." And like an unforeseen whirlwind he swept from the shop and marched off down the hill.

The relief at having got away with not telling the mayor their names, and not being pressed for this information, made Nancy feel quite weak.

"Oh dear," said Mrs Cavendish faintly. "I think I need a pot of tea and a lie-down."

"I'll make you one, Ma. You go and put your feet up," said Burch, putting an arm round his mother and giving her a quick kiss on the cheek.

"You are a good boy, Burch," his mother said, giving him a shaky smile.

"Come on, I'll see you out," Burch said, gesturing for Nancy to follow him.

Nancy thanked Mrs Cavendish for her help in cleaning and binding Violet's elbow.

"It's no trouble. Do stop by if you're passing again," Mrs Cavendish said with a distracted smile.

Outside the shop, Burch was staring down the street at the mayor's rapidly retreating back. Nancy watched the mayor pause and greet two women wearing church-black dresses and hats. His demeanour was easy and relaxed, as if his bad mood had been burned away by a ray of sunlight. He must have said something amusing, for the women's laughs echoed up the street.

"I'm sorry for the way the mayor treated your father," said Nancy, glancing at Violet, who was distracted by the objects in the haberdashery shop window. "He was perfectly beastly. He treats my grandfather horribly too. Quite the opposite of the way he's talking to those two women over there."

Burch's eyebrows pulled together just as they had when the mayor was in the shop. "The mayor spreads rumours about Mr Greenstone which I don't believe to be true, and he has my pa under his thumb." His jaw clenched as they stood in silence watching the mayor bid the women goodbye and continue to the end of Abbeygate Street. At the corner, the mayor turned and looked in their direction. It was too far away to see his expression, but Nancy was certain he was staring right at them.

"The mayor came into Grandfather's shop and said some terrible things about him selling tea infested with mouse droppings. Are those the sorts of rumour he's been spreading?" asked Nancy.

"Yes, they are just like that. Mr Greenstone's lost most of his customers because of it," said Burch with a frown.

"I don't understand why the mayor would say such things, and why he treats your father so badly," said Nancy, her cheeks burning with indignation.

"I don't know either, but wish I did. Then I might be able to do something about it," said Burch.

Nancy saw Burch's hands were still clenched and he seemed to be trembling.

"When are you next delivering to my grandfather's shop?" Nancy asked.

"Tomorrow morning, just after seven," Burch said. "Why do you ask?"

"I can't bear to see the mayor treating people like this. I don't have time to talk now as I must get Violet back to the house, but maybe there are things you can tell me that will help me work out what's going on," said Nancy.

Burch pushed his hands into his trouser pockets. "You think you can do something to help?"

"I've got to try," said Nancy firmly.

Burch nodded. "I could come an hour earlier tomorrow. Mr Greenstone's given me a key to the shop."

Nancy gave Burch a quick smile. If her grandfather trusted Burch with a key, she had a strong feeling she could trust him too, and she needed all the help she could get if she was to solve these mysteries.

CHAPTER 15

Herbal Remedy

Nancy and Violet arrived back at Cupola House to find a note from their mother under the salt cellar on the kitchen table saying she had gone back to bed with a thumping headache. On the ground floor, the smell of beeswax curled into the hall from the shop. Taking Violet's hand, Nancy led her sister inside, where their grandfather was polishing the counter with a yellow duster.

"Hello, girls," he said, looking up. "Did you enjoy the gardens?"

Nancy grimaced. "I'm afraid we didn't get that far."

"I hurt myself," said Violet, showing off her newly bound elbow.

"Oh," said Grandfather, frowning. He hurried over and looked at the bandage as Violet told him about the incident with the car. "I am glad it wasn't more serious. But where did this bandage come from?" he said, giving Nancy a nervous glance.

"Mrs Cavendish from the haberdashery helped us. And her son Burch. I saw him in the shop yesterday morning. He told us he's your delivery boy," said Nancy in a rush. She wished she could talk to her grandfather about the mayor and what Burch had said about him. But he might not be happy to learn she had talked to Burch so freely. "Mother said not to talk to anyone, but how could we not when people were so kind and we needed help?"

Grandfather sighed. "You did the right thing. Of course you had to accept the Cavendish family's help."

"But what shall we tell Mother? She will be so cross that Violet is hurt and that we disobeyed her instructions," said Nancy, wondering what the consequences of her and Violet speaking with Burch and his family might be. Mother had never shown this type of nervousness before.

Grandfather tapped on his chin, his eyes a little hazy. "Of course you should tell your mother about the accident, but perhaps she doesn't need to know the whole of it. Protecting those we love from unsettling truths is not always a bad thing."

Nancy stared at him. The thought of lying to their mother did not sit comfortably with her, but to tell the truth of their meeting with the Cavendish family (and the mayor!) might cause her more worry, as Grandfather had suggested, and she did not want that either.

"Now let me look at that elbow, Violet," their grandfather said, starting to unwind the bandage. "It seems you've had quite an adventure today."

"We saw the mayor too," Violet said suddenly.

"What?" Grandfather looked up. His eyes were suddenly glassy, even afraid.

Nancy pushed her hands into her apron pockets. Perhaps it was a good thing Violet had mentioned the mayor, for she hadn't known how to raise the subject. "The mayor treated poor Mr Cavendish terribly, made him polish his shoes while he was wearing them and work on his day of rest!"

Their grandfather looked aghast. "Percival Douglas is a man to be avoided. I made a mistake telling your mother it was all right for you to go out," he said worriedly, rubbing the ends of his moustache.

"Oh!" exclaimed Nancy. "Percival Douglas is the name written in an astronomy book Violet found in the cupola." What was the horrid mayor's book doing up there?

Grandfather looked at Nancy and Violet in astonishment. "Percival's book is still up there, after all these years?"

A thought occurred to Nancy. "Is *the mayor* something to do with the reason Mother wanted us to stay inside?" she asked, willing her grandfather to keep talking and shed some light on the gathering mysteries.

Violet leaned forward to listen as she nibbled on a thumbnail.

"You must keep away from him," said their grandfather, his eyes darkening.

"When was he in the cupola?" Nancy persisted.

"A long time ago, before things went so wrong," he replied, pushing his spectacles further up his nose and examining Violet's elbow.

"The mayor's been treating you terribly for ages then?" asked Nancy, horrified if this was the case.

Grandfather nodded.

"And that is the reason we have come to stay?" pressed Nancy.

"You are a perceptive child," Grandfather said softly, giving her a quick look.

Nancy hoped he would say more, but it was as if his lips had been suddenly sealed with glue. But his words had told her something important: the reason for their return, and their mother's jumpiness, *was* to do with the mayor.

"You know where the herbs are, Nancy dear. Bring me a little dried chickweed and we'll make a poultice for Violet's wound," her grandfather said, changing the subject. "It will help reduce the swelling."

"But can't we talk some more about the mayor?" asked Nancy hopefully.

"Yes, can't we?" said Violet.

"Please speak no more of that man, especially to your mother," their grandfather said, his forehead as furrowed as a concertina. "Is that clear, my dears?"

Violet nodded solemnly. She opened her mouth as if to say something, then closed it again.

"Yes, grandfather," said Nancy with a heavy sigh.

Nancy collected the chickweed as her grandfather had asked. They worked quietly together, grinding the dried leaves in a pestle and mortar and adding a little water until it formed a green paste, Nancy puzzling all the while over the discovery that the mean-spirited mayor had been in the cupola. She found it difficult to imagine her grandfather ever allowing the mayor into this house, no matter how persistent he was.

Her grandfather looked as if he had dropped into a well of misery and Nancy leaned across and tentatively patted him on the shoulder. He reached up and placed his hand over hers. His touch was warm and soft, but also weighted with sadness. He had tended to Violet so carefully, finding just the right herbal remedy to ease her sister's pain. Nancy wished there was a remedy in his shop that could make him feel better too.

CHAPTER 16

Night Watchers

That evening, Mother peeped round Nancy and Violet's bedroom door a little after ten o'clock, the light from her oil lamp flickering over the golden birds on the wallpaper so their wings appeared to take flight. "What are you still doing awake, Nancy? It's late," she whispered. "Did Violet settle? Her elbow wasn't too sore?" Mother had readily believed their story of Violet falling and tripping as they entered Cupola House after their walk.

Nancy noticed that her mother was dressed in the same dark-velvet cloak with the draping hood she had been wearing the night before. "Where are you going?" she whispered, slipping from the bed, walking over to her mother and stroking the fabric. It was as smooth as butter under her fingers. There was something sticking out of the right pocket of the cloak; another brown paper package.

Nancy's mother followed her gaze. She placed the lamp on a chest of drawers and pushed the package deep within the folds of the cloak until it was hidden. "I'm going out for a short walk, with your grandfather. We want to view the comet from the town square."

"But surely you would get a better view from the cupola, through the telescope?" whispered Nancy, trying to hide the suspicion in her voice, wondering why both her mother and grandfather were going out this time.

"Please don't question me, Nancy. You are old enough to stay at home alone and I need you to remain here with Violet. All the doors will be locked; you will be quite safe," her mother said.

Nancy dropped her head.

Her mother sighed. "I know this may all seem a little odd, darling. But I really am here to help your grandfather." She reached forward and stroked a strand of hair behind Nancy's ear and then pulled her into a fierce hug. Nancy was struck with the sudden memory of happier times at home. "We won't be out for long, I promise," her mother murmured into her hair, holding her so close it was as if she wanted to glue herself to Nancy and never let go. Then, dropping a quick kiss on the top of Nancy's head, her mother pulled away, picked up the lamp and swept down the stairs, the light illuminating the hem of her cloak like a slick of oil.

Nancy stood and listened as her grandfather murmured something to her mother, then shortly afterwards heard the judder of the back door closing from the depths of the house as they went out into the night. She and Violet were alone. A little shiver skittered over her shoulders. *There is no need to be afraid*, she told herself sternly as she listened to the creaks and groans of the house settling. This was just an old house made of bricks and mortar; there was nothing to fear.

She glanced at her sister, who was sleeping deeply. She had to find out where her grandfather and mother were going. And the cupola could be the answer! If they were going to the town square, she might catch a glimpse of them and the recipient of the package. It was also a chance to see what Grandfather had been looking at through the telescope. It seemed clear as day now that their visit was not to help their grandfather watch the comet because of his poor health. Mother had not been telling them the truth. For one thing, why would they take a package outside with them to comet watch? But she *had* learned today that their visit was connected with the mayor. Perhaps the mysterious packages were for him, but if that was the case why deliver them at night? Trepidation bubbled in Nancy's chest as she slipped quietly out of the bedroom and onto the landing, walked past the silently watching herbs and oils and ran up the stairs to the observatory on top of the roof.

Being inside the cupola during the day felt like being on the top of a mountain, at night it felt even more so. Ordinarily Nancy thought she might have seen the glow of lights from the town bleeding into the darkening sky, but tonight with the comet in view, many homes were dark. She could see some windows were flung wide as people leaned out and looked to the skies, some even perching on rooftops and balancing on ledges. These were the people who were not afraid of the gaseous comet, but were trying to get a view of it burning across the sky before it reached its closest point to Earth in three days' time and then started to fade.

A small thrill caused Nancy to clench her toes into the floorboards as she joined the other night watchers looking above the rooftops. Faint shouts came from all directions, people telling one another, "Look up, look up!" Nancy kneeled on the bench and placed a palm on the arched window which overlooked the town square. There were a few people milling around and looking up at the comet, but there was no sight of her mother, in her long cloak, or her grandfather.

She watched for a few minutes more, her eyes straining in the dark. She sighed and turned to look at the telescope, which was facing out of the opposite window. It was still pointing at the rooftops rather than the sky. Bending to look through the eyepiece, she was greeted with a fuzzy black nothingness. She dimly remembered her father's small telescope, which she and Violet were sometimes allowed to take into their tiny back garden on a summer night if there was a full moon. It had a knob to bring the view into focus. Looking up from the eyepiece, Nancy quickly found the focuser and looked through the telescope again. She turned the knob slowly. Sure enough the fuzziness began to recede, revealing pinpricks of light. As her eyes adjusted still further, she saw that the telescope was pointing to the top of a tall, castle-like crenellated wall, beyond which was a yard and another even taller building. She pulled the telescope down a little until she was looking at the street.

Two people were standing in front of the wall, their heads bowed as they talked. The smaller of the figures was wearing a long cloak which brushed the ground. Nancy pulled away from the eyepiece and blinked hard. *It was Mother and Grandfather.* Looking through the eyepiece again she waited for her sight to readjust. But the figures had disappeared. She moved the telescope slowly to the left, until she saw two large wooden doors and a sign above it illuminated by a street lamp: *Town Gaol.* Nancy stood back from the eyepiece and rubbed her eyes until the stars she saw behind them were blurred, just like the comet in the sky. What possible business did her mother and grandfather have at the town prison? The mysteries were mounting and she decided there and then to talk them over with Burch when he came to the shop early the next morning, for she needed to get some answers.

CHAPTER 17

Anti-comet Pills

Nancy heard her mother and grandfather return to Cupola House around an hour after leaving on their mysterious night-time errand. She had slept fitfully after that, images of telescopes and jagged prison walls and a woman in a long dark cloak spinning around in her head on an endless loop. She finally got out of bed as dawn approached and, after quickly getting dressed and checking that Violet was still asleep, went downstairs to the apothecary shop to wait for Burch.

She kept herself busy by sweeping the already-clean

shop floor and polishing the display cabinets, bottles and jars until they shone, anxious to do anything to make her grandfather's life a little easier, while thinking about what to say to Burch. She would start by asking him whether he had any idea about the cause of her grandfather's bad relationship with the mayor. Getting to the root of a problem usually provided answers.

Just before six o'clock, a key turned in the lock and Burch opened the door cautiously, the bell thankfully emitting only a feeble tinkle, as if protesting at the early hour. He carried a box and another bag of provisions into the shop and his lips tilted into a smile as he saw Nancy waiting by the counter. She hurried across to take the bag, the smell of freshly baked bread making her stomach groan.

"How's Violet? Is she recovered from her accident?" said Burch quietly, placing the box on the countertop.

"She's all right. It was just a bad graze. I think the whole event tired her out. Thank you for bringing the provisions," Nancy said, placing the bag next to the box on the counter. The label on the box was printed in black lettering.

ANTI-COMET PILLS

A REMEDY TO ESCAPE THE ANGER OF THE
HEAVENS. MANUFACTURED IN THE USA.

This is what the silvery-haired people on the train three days earlier had been talking about; a pill which would prevent you from being poisoned by the cyanogen gas in the comet's tail.

"Do you believe we need to take these pills?" asked Nancy.

Burch frowned. "A few folks have been rattled by this comet, believing the terrible prophecies. My teacher, Mr Watts, told us of a newspaper report saying the comet would cause the Pacific and Atlantic oceans to boil when Earth passes through its tail this week, and some people who live near the big lakes in America are leaving their homes in case there's a tidal wave."

Nancy grimaced. "That does seem a bit silly."

"It does," said Burch. "I agree with Mr Watts that these reports are made by sensationalists, not scientists. Do you learn about practical science at your school, Nancy?"

Nancy wrinkled her nose. "My girls' school would never teach us anything like that. We do nature observations, but they are always rather boring, apart from the time someone found an ants' nest in the playground and brought it into the classroom."

Burch grinned. "Mr Watts has given us lessons on the storage of electricity and the dynamo – a mechanical device that can *make* electricity."

"Gosh," said Nancy enviously. "That does sound interesting. At my school last week our teacher lectured us on how we must walk with straight backs and tall necks and have pretty hair so that we'll make good wives."

Burch's grin widened. "That's not much of an aspiration."

"Wanting to be a wife is fine if that's what you choose, but it's certainly not my only aspiration," said Nancy, smiling too. "My father's a solicitor and I think it might be an interesting profession, that is, if women are ever allowed to work in law."

"It doesn't seem fair," said Burch, shaking his head. "My ma and pa both work in the haberdashery – well they did until Pa started working for the mayor – so why should it be different for any other profession?"

"I don't know. It doesn't make much sense to me either," said Nancy with a sigh.

"If I had a choice, I would be a scientist. Mr Watts

has given me a passion for it. He says scientists have examined the light radiating through Halley's comet for the first time. This tells them it is made of particles of ice, rock and gas. He says it's no threat to us at all. I believe him. I was hoping our school could visit the town observatory at the Subscription Rooms to view the comet, but the mayor says the telescope is broken," said Burch, his cheeks flushed, his voice animated.

"That's a pity. I remember the mayor mentioning the observatory when he came into your family's shop," said Nancy, feeling a growing affinity with Burch. He spoke rationally and had solid ideas, like her own father. "Speaking of the mayor, I wondered if I could ask what you know about him and my grandfather, and why there is such bad feeling between them?" she said, thinking of the people her father had defended and spoken of in the past. Yes, some people could just be horrid because they were mean-spirited, but her father said there was usually a strong reason why people treated others unjustly.

"I'm afraid I don't know the answer to that. Many folks in this town haven't got a bad word to say about the mayor. He can be charming and persuasive and Ma reckons this gets him voted in year after year," said

Burch, who Nancy noticed was now staring at the box of anti-comet pills on the counter.

"What is it?" asked Nancy.

"There is something I *do* know about Mr Greenstone and the mayor. Come and look at this," Burch said, walking to the storeroom at the back of the shop. Nancy followed, feeling a pinch of curiosity. Opening the door, Burch pointed to a stack of boxes to the rear, similar to the one on the counter. On the side of each box was the same black stamp. ANTI-COMET PILLS.

One of the boxes was open, straw spilling from its insides like a scarecrow. Nancy stepped into the storeroom, reached inside the box and pulled out a small jar of white pills. She turned and looked at Burch. "I don't understand. Why does my grandfather have so many of these? He has no customers and wouldn't want them for himself, so who are they for?"

Burch lowered his voice to a whisper. "Mr Greenstone heard that the mayor was looking to buy some anti-comet pills. He's been buying up the orders meant for other chemist shops in this town, and some as far away as Newmarket and Ipswich. He seems determined that the mayor shan't get his hands on them."

"So that is why the mayor asked whether you had

made any deliveries to the chemist shops yesterday?" said Nancy, remembering the mayor's question and Burch's nervous answer.

Burch nodded. "I reckon Mr Greenstone's trying to hurt the mayor in some small way to get back at him. The rumours the mayor spreads about Mr Greenstone's shop have been going on for years. It's got so bad that other shopkeepers and past customers want nothing to do with your grandfather. He doesn't like leaving the house, even asked for my help to bring his potted plants inside a few years back to avoid the whispers and looks. That's why I bring provisions, for I worry he'd starve if I didn't. I make my deliveries early, so people don't see what I am up to, for if the mayor got to hear of it…" Burch's voice trailed off.

"Thank you for being so kind to my grandfather," said Nancy, returning the jar of pills to the box and feeling a familiar burn of anger and confusion twist in her gut. "I'm sure the mayor is the reason we have come to stay." She walked back out into the shop, quickly telling Burch of the things she had learned over the past few days. The discovery that the mayor had been in the cupola at some point in the past. The night-time packages her mother and grandfather had been delivering, and where she had seen them through the telescope the previous night.

"But what would the mayor have to do with your mother and grandfather being outside the prison?" asked Burch, following her and leaning against the shop counter.

"I don't know," said Nancy, standing next to him.

Burch looked at Nancy for a few seconds then tapped on his chin. "You say the telescope was pointing to the prison when you looked through it last night?"

Nancy nodded.

"And it seems that your ma and Mr Greenstone are watching the prison from the cupola, as well as visiting it?" said Burch.

"But why do that?" asked Nancy, biting on her bottom lip.

Burch's frown deepened. "It's a mystery all right."

A small ball of determination was growing inside Nancy. She had been whisked away to this house and presented with a new and very troubled grandfather. Her mother was changing before her eyes into someone she didn't recognize and no one seemed to realize the unsettling effect all of this was having on her and Violet. "Mother and grandfather may go out again tonight. How about we follow them and see if these packages *are* being delivered to the prison? Maybe then we can find out who they are for and how the mayor is involved in all this," said Nancy. She wrinkled her nose. "Oh. But I can't leave Violet alone in the house."

"I could follow them on my own, come back here afterwards and tell you what I've found out?" offered Burch.

Nancy threw him a grateful smile. "Yes, that's a good plan. I do need to get to the bottom of what's going on."

"It feels good to be helping your family, even if I can't work out a way to help my own pa. Ever since he began assisting the mayor with the comet party preparations and collecting the ticket money he's not been himself, but when I question him about it he refuses to talk. The mayor knocked on our door late yesterday evening looking for Pa. He'd gone out for a pint of ale, so the mayor wrote him a note and asked me to pass it on to him."

Burch pulled at his collar and Nancy noticed his cheeks were a little pink. "Did you…read the note?" she asked hesitantly.

Burch grimaced. "I did. I felt bad for doing it, but couldn't stop myself as I thought it might give me some answers."

"And did it?" asked Nancy hopefully.

Burch shook his head. "No. The mayor told Pa to collect him from his house at eight-thirty this morning and drive him to the Subscription Rooms. He said he had an urgent task he wanted to discuss."

"Could it be something to do with preparing for the comet party?" asked Nancy with a frown.

"Perhaps. Although the mayor's never called on Pa so late, or passed on a note before," said Burch, his forehead creasing too.

Nancy felt a flutter in her chest. "I suppose you'll be at school, but if I can persuade Mother to let me and Violet go for a walk after breakfast, we could follow the mayor and your father into the Subscription Rooms, see if we can find out what this task is," said Nancy.

Burch's eyes widened. "Are you sure? But what if the mayor sees you?"

Nancy swallowed. It was a risk, but one she was prepared to take to help her new friend. "I'll be careful. I need to do something, Burch. I can't just sit around here all day watching these strange things happen. We both need answers and, one way or another, today we shall find them."

CHAPTER 18

Stay Inside

An hour or so after Burch had left the shop, Nancy's mother and grandfather came downstairs to the kitchen to find Violet sitting at the table, which was laden with plates of fried bacon, hard-boiled alabaster-white duck eggs and bread cut into thick slices.

"What is this?" her mother asked in bemusement.

"You were still in bed, so I decided to make breakfast," Nancy said as she washed up the pans. It was true that she wanted to help and be useful, but making breakfast had also eased a little of her guilt at the mounting secrets she was keeping from her mother

– not telling her about the mayor and sneaking up to the cupola to look through the telescope, not to mention the plans to follow her mother and grandfather as well as trying to to learn more about the task the mayor had for Burch's father.

"My delivery boy must have come early. You found the provisions in the shop?" asked Grandfather, peering at Nancy over the top of his spectacles.

Nancy placed the frying pan on the draining board and quickly dried her hands on a cloth. "Yes. They were next to a box of anti-comet pills," she said, not liking that she also had to hide her meeting with Burch from her grandfather.

"What are anti-comet pills?" asked Violet, who was eating her second egg and third slice of bread and butter.

"Nothing you need to worry yourself about," said their grandfather gruffly. "They are worthless nonsense, made of sugar paste. I shan't be selling them to anyone."

Hoarding the anti-comet pills might be one small triumph over the mayor, but why would her grandfather not stand up to him properly, or tell the police? Surely the bullying he was subjected to was on the wrong side of the law? Nancy wished that her father was there so she could ask him.

Grandfather walked to the range, picked up the copper kettle and began to prepare a pot of tea.

"Please may we take a walk again this morning, Mother?" asked Nancy, leaning back against the sink and crossing her fingers behind her back for luck.

"Oh, please can we! I promise I won't fall today," said Violet, through a mouthful of bread.

Mother had sat at the table and was staring at her empty plate in a vacant manner. "No, not today," she said looking up.

Nancy blinked, took a step forward. "But why? You let us go out yesterday."

"And that was a mistake," said Mother, glancing at Violet's elbow.

"Please," began Nancy, her arms dropping to her sides.

"No," said Mother. "My mind is made up. You can stay inside and sew your handkerchiefs."

Violet slumped in her chair.

Nancy's stomach clenched. She did not want to let Burch down. "But, Mother…" she persisted.

"Nancy!" exclaimed Mother, her eyes suddenly looking as if they could shoot fire. "That is enough!"

Heat flashed up Nancy's back. "I'm…sorry," she said, lowering her head. Her lips trembled. If only she hadn't stopped to look at the comet poster in town yesterday, or been distracted by the two men talking outside the wine shop. If only Violet hadn't skipped off. If those things hadn't happened then Violet would not have fallen and Mother would most likely have allowed them outside again. But at least everything that had happened had led her to meet Burch. She swallowed back her tears. She needed to accept her plan for the morning had been thwarted, but it did not make the injustice of the fact she was only trying to help any easier to bear.

There was sudden thumping above their heads. Grandfather looked to the basement stairs, a cloud crossing his face. He placed the teapot on the table, a little liquid spilling from the spout as his hands trembled. "A shop customer," he said gruffly, heading to the door.

Mother mopped up the tea without comment and Violet munched on her bread, watching their mother warily. Nancy heard Grandfather's feet on the stairs, the groan of the internal door to the shop opening. A short while later the jangle of the bell as someone entered the shop. But surely it was still too early for customers?

"May I be excused?" asked Nancy in a small voice.

Her mother nodded, not looking up from the bread she was now buttering.

Curiosity drew Nancy from the kitchen to the stairs.

"Good day, Mr Greenstone."

The insincere greeting trickled into her ears like scuttling beetles. *The mayor.* She glanced back at Mother and Violet, but they were talking. Pulling the door to the kitchen closed, Nancy quickly ran up the stairs and stood with her ear to the shop door.

"What can I do for you, Mayor?" asked her grandfather, his voice as taut as wire rope. "You have taken away my customers and destroyed my reputation. Why visit me again today? What more do you want from me?"

Nancy pressed her ear so firmly to the door it ached.

"I think you know very well why I have come to visit you again. And I want the same thing I wanted from the very beginning," the mayor said in a low voice.

There was a short silence.

"That is the one thing you shall never have," said Nancy's grandfather. Another pause stretched like rubber and Nancy stiffened as she waited for the mayor to respond.

"Things could have been different," said the mayor. "If only you had kept your word. Your daughter…"

"Don't speak of my daughter," said Grandfather in a sharp tone that Nancy had not heard before.

"She got what she deserved," said the mayor in a sudden wolflike snarl.

Nancy placed her palms flat against the door. The mayor was talking about her mother.

"The terms you set out in the letter. I stuck to them. Please. Please just leave us…me…alone," pleaded Nancy's grandfather.

"That. Will. Never. Happen," said the mayor with the force of a flying arrow. "Especially now."

"I can't think what you mean by that," said her grandfather nervously.

"Oh, yes you can, Mr Greenstone. You know perfectly well what I mean. I shall be in touch." There was the stomp of footsteps and the clang of the shop bell as the mayor left the premises.

Nancy heard the sound of the key being turned in the shop door. She listened for a second more. "How does he know? Something must be done," Nancy heard her grandfather mutter. "Something must be done," he said again.

The longcase clock in the hallway ticked in time with Nancy's breaths. The gargoyles on the bannister waited and watched with eager eyes. She knocked tentatively on the door. "Grandfather?" she called. "Is everything all right?"

"Nancy? How long have you been out there?" Grandfather asked, his voice far away, as if he had curled up into a corner.

"Um…not long," said Nancy, thinking it best he didn't know what she had overheard.

"Good. All is well. I will be down shortly," Grandfather replied weakly.

Nancy walked upstairs to her bedroom, her fingers trailing over the polished bannister. The mayor saying her mother had got what she deserved brought an unpleasant heaviness to her limbs. What had he meant by that? He had also mentioned wanting something, and Grandfather had said he would never have it. Was this connected to the packages Mother and Grandfather had been taking out at night? She couldn't physically help Burch follow them to see if they *were* taking them to the prison, but she was mentally filing away the new things she had learned to share with him, as she was certain they provided clues to what was happening.

Stepping into the bedroom, Nancy heard the mayor's raised voice on the street outside from her half-open window. Her instinct was to rush to the window, pull back the curtains and peer out. But if Mother's wariness about them being seen was because of the mayor, perhaps she needed to be more cautious. Hiding herself behind the curtains, she peeped down into the quiet street, where she saw a shiny red motor car and the mayor standing beside it. On his knees polishing the car was Burch's father, wearing his chauffeur's cap. Nancy saw the mayor's head twitch in displeasure and felt a pull in her chest.

"Each time we make a stop the car must be spotless by the time I return, Cavendish. I fear your work is becoming slapdash. I do hope you and your wife don't run the haberdashery with the same poor attention to detail. If word of that got around, you might lose customers." The mayor's voice, which was bright and challenging, ought to have drawn attention from anyone passing. But the few people around kept their heads down and walked on, as if the unfolding scene wasn't happening at all. "Drive me to the Subscription Rooms. I must tell you about the task I have for you," the mayor continued, in a lower voice than before.

Mr Cavendish looked up at the mayor, his cheeks flushed scarlet and strained with misery.

Nancy stood away from the window. The mayor was threatening Burch's father. He was awful to her grandfather. The two men providing food and wine for the mayor's comet party seemed to dislike him too. He had a hold over the people in this town that had to be stopped; bullies and liars could not be allowed to win.

CHAPTER 19

Followed

"I'm not a bit tired," said Violet that evening. "Why does Mother make us go to bed so early?"

"Perhaps because she is tired herself," said Nancy. It was a little after eight o'clock and it was true that Mother had asked them to prepare for bed particularly early that evening after their day of endless needlework. Her eyes were distracted and far away as she poured warm water into the washstand, brought in clean commodes and placed them beneath the beds. Was this because she wanted them asleep before going out on another mysterious night-time errand with their grandfather? Nancy hoped so, for then at least Burch would be able to follow them and discover whether they were delivering the packages to the prison. If they could somehow find out who the packages were intended for, might the recipient be able to shed some light on what was happening?

"I miss Father reading to me at bedtime," said Violet, rolling onto her side and slipping her hands under her cheek. "We were in the middle of *The Wind in the Willows*, the part where Mole goes into the Wild Wood to try and meet Badger."

"I miss Father too," said Nancy. "But Mother said we would be going home after the comet has reached its peak. That happens the day after tomorrow, so I can't imagine we will be here much longer." But while Nancy was also missing home, there was a large part of her that did not want to return to Leeds and leave their grandfather alone in this big house without unravelling the mysteries surrounding their visit.

"Do you think we have come to stay because of the mayor?" asked Violet.

"Why do you say that?" asked Nancy in surprise. Her sister's cheeks were pinched and a little pale. Perhaps she had been more unsettled than Nancy had realized at the mayor's treatment of Burch's father in the haberdashery shop, and by what their grandfather had said.

Violet opened her mouth as if she were about to say something else then closed it again and sniffed.

"How about I read to you?" said Nancy, hoping that this might banish all thoughts of the mayor from her sister's mind.

Violet looked up. "But you never read to me any more at home. Not since you moved to the bedroom upstairs."

Nancy felt a burn of guilt. There had been a time when she and Violet had regularly snuggled in bed together, pressing their cold toes against each other's legs as they pored over the pages of a book. But since moving to her own room she often forgot about Violet's bedtime.

"Wait here. I'll be back in a minute," said Nancy, getting out of bed. She returned a short while later with the *Merry Rhymes* book from the attic bedroom. Climbing into bed with Violet, she smoothed the covers over their legs. As she opened the book and began to read, Violet snuggled into Nancy's side. The rhymes were childish, meant for children much younger, but Violet didn't seem to mind, and Nancy found to her surprise that she didn't either. It was warm and comforting sitting pressed close together, and she made a silent resolution to do this more often when they returned home, whenever that may be.

Once Violet was soundly asleep, Nancy placed the book on the bedside table and went and stood by the bedroom door and listened, hoping to hear the sounds of her mother and grandfather preparing to go out. She rubbed her eyes, which were gritty with tiredness. Thankfully she did not have to wait for long.

"Are you sure this is the right thing to do?" Nancy heard her grandfather ask when the sky had fully darkened.

"It is an opportunity we cannot ignore. You said yourself that something must be done, and I cannot stand by any longer," replied Nancy's mother.

Nancy heard ten gentle chimes from the clock on the landing, the sound of feet on the stairs and a short while later the thud of the basement door. She flew to the window and carefully pulled back the curtain. Burch was standing under a street lamp near the fire station looking up at the house, just as they had arranged. He must have noticed the movement at her window, for he gave a quick nod and set off down the street in pursuit of her mother and grandfather.

Nancy turned up the oil lamp and crept downstairs to wait in the kitchen, the spare key to the back door clenched in her hot palm. She heard the occasional call from the comet watchers outside.

"It's brighter tonight!"

"Do you see the flare in the comet's tail?"

"Only two days until the comet party. It's sure to be the event of the year."

Around twenty minutes later there was a rap on the kitchen door. "It's me," Burch said in a low voice.

Nancy quickly unlocked the door and opened it.

Burch was breathless as he emerged from the shadows.

"Did you see where they went? Was it to the prison?" Nancy whispered, beckoning him inside.

Burch shook his head glumly as he walked into the kitchen.

Nancy locked the door behind him and replaced the key on the hook. "What happened?"

"I was following them at a distance, but they weren't

going in the direction of the prison. Then I bumped into my pa on his way out for a pint of ale. By the time I'd finished speaking with him, I'd lost sight of Mr Greenstone and your ma. I walked past the prison twice, but there was no one around."

Nancy made a quick decision, a heady combination of nerves and excitement causing her stomach to knot. "We'll go to the cupola and look from up there."

Burch glanced at the door. "But what if they come back?"

"Come on, we'll be quick. They were gone for an hour the other night," urged Nancy, picking up the oil lamp.

"Well…if you're sure," said Burch, looking to the back door one final time then following Nancy, whose footsteps were already creaking up the stairs.

Nancy heard Burch give a low whistle as he walked behind her into the cupola. She extinguished the oil lamp and placed it on the floor. The comet was burning across the sky, seeming closer than ever before.

Burch placed a palm on one of the windows. "Have you ever seen anything like it?" he whispered. "When Edmond Halley the astronomer saw this comet in the 1600s, he worked out it had an orbit and would keep on returning. Historians looked back at old pictures and books and found it to be true, even discovered that William the Conqueror might have seen it at the Battle of Hastings in 1066."

"Gosh. I didn't know that," admitted Nancy, stepping over to the telescope. When this comet next made an appearance, it would be the year 1986, a year so far into the future she could not begin to imagine it.

"I wish I could stay on at school, learn more about such things," said Burch, peering through the glass to the sky.

"Why can't you?" asked Nancy.

"Ma's busier than ever in the haberdashery since Pa began working for the mayor. She needs my help and wants me to leave school at the end of the year," Burch replied with a sigh.

Nancy felt an arrow of sympathy for Burch. Her own parents were big supporters of education and she could not imagine being told she must leave school and start work.

"Mother made us stay inside today, so I didn't find out what task the mayor had for your father. I am sorry," said Nancy regretfully.

"No matter. But thanks for offering to help," said

Burch. "It was probably something to do with the comet party in any case."

"I suppose," said Nancy, looking through the eyepiece of the telescope, and adjusting the focus knob as she had done before. She pulled away in surprise.

"What is it?" asked Burch.

"You look," said Nancy, stepping to one side. The telescope was not pointing at the prison. This time it was giving a direct and rather incredible close-up view of the comet. The great sword of diffused light bleeding across the inky sky seemed close enough to touch. The beauty of it caused Nancy to sit on a bench with a heavy thump.

Burch stood up and looked through the eyepiece. He gasped, reaching out a finger in the direction the telescope was pointing as if trying to touch what he could see. "The comet," he whispered. "It's huge. I can see the nucleus – it's the shape of a potato. I wish Mr Watts could see this." He pulled his eye away from the telescope and sat next to her. "Whoever was up here last was watching the comet, Nancy, not the prison."

Nancy curled her fingers into the velvet seat-cushion. Had she been mistaken in thinking that her grandfather and mother were watching and visiting the prison?

Burch had certainly not seen them going towards the prison tonight. Where *had* they been going? Her thoughts were hazy and she closed her eyes for a second. "The mayor came into my grandfather's shop again this morning. I think he visits often," she said after a while. "He mentioned wanting something that my grandfather said he would never have. Then the mayor said my mother got what she deserved. Don't you think that sounds awful? What do you think it all means?"

Burch frowned. "I don't know. What could the mayor want?"

Nancy looked around the cupola and thought of the astronomy book Violet had found that belonged to the mayor. She glanced at the brass telescope. "Grandfather said the telescope is an antique. Could it be valuable?"

Burch shook his head. "The mayor's a rich man; he could buy any telescope he wanted. And if he enjoyed watching the night sky surely he'd have made more of an effort to mend the telescope in the town observatory?"

Nancy sighed. It seemed like an impossible puzzle: a tangle of conversations and secrets that had no answer.

There was a sudden clanking noise from the street below, the sound of shouts. "Fire...there's a fire."

Nancy and Burch looked at one another. Leaping to their feet, they peered from one of the cupola windows down to the fire station. Horses were being harnessed to the fire cart. "You don't have a motorized fire engine in this town?" asked Nancy, her eyes widening.

"No," said Burch. "If we did, that *would* be a sight to see."

The horses clattered down the street, pulling the fire cart behind them, as a fireman rang a bell to clear a way through the comet watchers.

"I wonder where the fire is?" said Burch. "I don't see any smoke."

Far below, in the depths of Cupola House a door banged.

Nancy stared at Burch with a mounting horror as two sets of footsteps could be heard climbing the stairs. "Mother and Grandfather are back," she whispered.

Burch's jaw twitched. "I can't be caught up here!"

Nancy cast her eyes wildly around the small octagonal room. They were trapped at the top of the house with no means of escape. What on earth were they to do? An idea burst into her head like a firework. Gesturing for Burch to stand up, she quickly pulled up one of the velvet bench-cushions.

Burch looked at her with a sudden understanding. It was the only option. Folding his long limbs as small as he could, he clambered into the bench like a hermit crab squeezing into a tiny shell. Nancy replaced the cushion with trembling hands. "Stay hidden until you are sure they are in bed," she said quietly, telling him where to find the key to the back door. He gave a quick rap on the underside of the bench, signalling that he understood.

Taking one last quick look around the cupola to make sure things were just the same as when they had arrived, Nancy picked up the oil lamp, ran lightly down the two flights of stairs and into her room. Turning down the lamp, she jumped into her bed and pulled the covers up to her neck, her limbs tingling.

Minutes later she heard the creak of her bedroom door and sensed the presence of her mother. "All is well," she heard her mother whisper, quietly closing the door again.

"I told you they would be fine," her grandfather murmured. "Now we just need to wait. I hope the mayor agrees to this, Charlotte. For I am at the end of my tether."

Nancy heard the sound of two pairs of feet retreating

up the stairs and the creaks of the floorboards in the bedrooms above. Her head spinning, Nancy stared at the wall in the dark, her ears pricked and alert for the sound of Burch leaving as she desperately tried to piece the puzzle together. Mother and Grandfather had been to visit the mayor. Was that to ask him to leave their family alone? But she still didn't know the cause of the bad feeling in the first place. And how did the watching of the prison and the strange packages fit in with this? Her frustrations at having to follow rules of obedience, staying quiet, keeping out of sight and not being able to solve these mysteries herself, were making her skin hot and prickly.

She rolled onto her back and stared at the ceiling. Mother's eyes would narrow with disapproval, but Nancy knew she must confront her first thing in the morning and persist until she had some answers. She would have to admit to listening in on conversations and sneaking around, but she was prepared to take whatever punishment she was given. She listened to the creaks and groans of the house as her mother and grandfather prepared to go to bed, hearing the soft whinny of horses as the fire cart returned across the street. A short while later Burch's footsteps could be heard on the stairs, and with the decision made to seek answers from her mother the next day, Nancy at last fell into a deep and dreamless sleep.

CHAPTER 20

Police

Nancy woke with a jump to find Violet standing over her, shaking her shoulder. She sat up and rubbed her eyes.

"Someone's banging at the shop door," said Violet anxiously, pulling on Nancy's arm. "I heard shouting so went downstairs. They said to open up. It's the police."

Leaping out of bed, Nancy ran to the window, gingerly parting the curtains to peep down to the street below. Two policemen in black helmets stood on the shop doorstep. *Bang, bang, bang, bang.* "Open up, Mr Greenstone," one of them shouted.

Nancy let the curtains drop from her fingers in alarm.

"What in heaven's name is happening?" Nancy heard her mother call.

Nancy flung open their bedroom door. Her mother was tying the cord of her dressing gown round her waist as she stood on the first-floor landing.

"Wait, Charlotte. I'll go," her grandfather called out, appearing a few seconds later in his nightshirt. They both continued down to the ground floor, not paying Nancy or Violet the slightest attention.

Nancy felt a quell of nausea as she followed them downstairs. Her mother was hovering in the ground-floor hallway.

"No…she's not here," she heard her grandfather say from within the shop.

"We have witnesses," said a voice – one of the policemen.

"But I live alone, have done for years," said her grandfather.

"Don't try and pull the wool over our eyes, Mr Greenstone. If you don't fetch your daughter right this minute, we will be forced to search the house." The policeman's voice was low and determined and meant business.

Nancy saw her mother shift position. She glanced up the stairs and Nancy shrank back into the shadows, but she had been seen. Nancy was about to go downstairs when her mother raised a hand, instructing her to stay where she was. She touched a finger to her lips signalling for Nancy to be quiet, then she was gone, walking into the shop.

"I am here," Nancy heard her mother say. "There is no need to search the house."

Nancy lowered herself slowly until she was sitting on the stairs. She pulled her knees close to her chest and hugged them.

"Miss Greenstone, you have returned," one of the policemen said in surprise. Her mother didn't reply.

"A return which almost had rather devastating consequences for Mayor Douglas last night," said a different, more gravelly voice – the other policeman.

"The mayor?" her grandfather said. "What does he have to do with your visit?"

"As if you don't know," said the first policeman, in an unpleasant sneering tone. "Miss Greenstone, I am arresting you for attempted arson – for trying to burn down the mayor's house. I need you to accompany me to the police station for questioning."

Nancy felt the hair lift at the nape of her neck. "Arson?" she whispered. Their mother had tried to burn down the mayor's house? She heard a creak and looked up to see Violet creeping downstairs. She came and sat next to Nancy, so close their arms bumped together. Nancy clasped her knees tightly, waiting for Mother to tell the policemen they had made the most dreadful mistake.

"Tell them, Charlotte. Tell them you did not do this," urged their grandfather.

"We have a witness," said the gravelly voiced policeman. "And evidence." There was a pause. "You were seen pushing a burning handkerchief through the mayor's letter box last night…a little after ten in the evening."

"No!" exclaimed their grandfather. "That is not what happened!"

Violet dragged in a sharp breath and reached for Nancy's hand.

This was ridiculous. Their mother was the wife of an upstanding solicitor and pillar of the local community. She attended church each week in Leeds. Said grace before mealtimes. She was not an arsonist. With all of her being, Nancy willed her mother to speak up and defend herself.

"Charlotte Greenstone…I am arresting you for the…"

"Yes, yes," said her mother sharply, finding her voice at last. "I heard your accusation the first time. I haven't used the name Greenstone for many years. I am Mrs Rivers now. You have a case of mistaken identity. Now please leave."

One of the policemen barked out a snarling laugh that made Nancy shiver. She pressed her palm into her sister's hand and gave Violet what she hoped was a reassuring look.

"Do you happen to own any handkerchiefs with red-ribbon edging?" the policeman said. "They are very distinctive…and we have it on good authority that you sew these handkerchiefs yourself."

There was a long pause. *One of the handkerchiefs that Nancy and her mother embroidered had been used to commit the crime. But how could that be?*

"Yes, it sounds like one of mine but…" began their mother.

"And were you, or were you not, in the vicinity of the mayor's house just after ten o'clock last night?" interrupted the policeman.

A heavy silence settled on the house.

"Careful now, *Miss Greenstone*. Remember, we have a witness," said the deep-voiced policeman, as triumphantly as if he'd just caught a fish he had been trying to hook all day.

"Yes, I was there but…" said their mother tightly.

"There we have it then," said the other policeman. "What a sorry situation. Mr Greenstone, you may fetch your daughter's coat, then we are taking her to the police station."

"May I please get dressed first?" requested Mother, her voice trembling a little.

"No time for that," replied the policeman.

Nancy bit hard on her bottom lip. *This couldn't be happening.*

"Mayor Douglas," their mother said in a small voice. "Is he…was he…hurt?"

The air in the hallway seemed to constrict, squeezing Nancy's lungs. Violet smothered a small gasp.

"No. It is lucky the witness to the crime banged on his door to alert him," said one of the policemen. "If he had perished you would be facing a far worse charge."

Pinches of dread needled at Nancy's skin as she realized that their mother was being arrested for an unimaginable crime, and that she had not protested her innocence. The mysteries she was facing had suddenly taken the most terrible and dangerous turn.

CHAPTER 21

Arrested

Through their bedroom window Nancy and Violet watched their mother being led from Cupola House, flanked by the two policemen. It was still early in the morning and the few people about pointed and whispered as their mother was marched down the street, the hem of her dressing gown billowing out from beneath her coat like a sail on a stormy sea.

Violet was pale-faced and silent. She clambered back into her bed and pulled the covers up to her wobbling chin.

Nancy wished she could do the same, but she was

the eldest and had to look after her sister. Perhaps she should say the words she hoped would turn out to be true. "It will be all right, Violet," she soothed, with more conviction than she felt. "The police will soon realize they have made a terrible mistake. Of course Mother didn't try to burn down the mayor's house."

Violet didn't reply. In fact, she looked positively doubtful.

There was a quiet knock at their bedroom door. Their grandfather stepped tentatively inside. His hair was in tufty peaks, and beads of sweat peppered his forehead.

"We heard everything," said Nancy, striding over to him.

Grandfather's eyes narrowed. "This is my fault," he whispered. "If only I had not written to your mother and asked her to come…"

"Why *did* you invite her here?" asked Nancy, unable to keep the tremor from her voice. "I know this is to do with the mayor and that the two of you have been going out, delivering packages at night. You were near the mayor's house last night. But why would he accuse Mother of arson? It doesn't make sense."

Their grandfather lowered his head and rubbed his

wan cheeks. "Nancy, my dear. I am so sorry this has happened. I must go and think how to unpick this mess, make things right."

"But we can't just leave Mother with the police. We need to *do* something. Should we...contact our father?" Nancy asked hesitantly.

"No, not yet," Grandfather said, his voice suddenly weary. "This is my doing so I must resolve matters. Try not to worry yourselves. I'll...I'll come downstairs when I've had time to think. Please stay inside and keep the doors locked." And with that he walked limply from the room and up the stairs, the slam of his bedroom door reverberating through the house.

Nancy sat on the edge of her bed, fear and uncertainty causing her to shiver. She heard the rumble of Violet's stomach and saw she was nibbling on a thumbnail. Her sister looked so forlorn. "I think there are still some crumpets in the larder. Father always says decisions made on empty stomachs are never good ones," said Nancy, trying to force some brightness into her voice. *Their father.* Should she heed her grandfather's wishes and not contact him about these troubling events? But surely he would want to know and be able to help? Their grandfather did not have a telephone and she had no money to go to the post office to send a telegram. She bit hard on her bottom lip. *Burch.* He would know what to do, but it was Tuesday and a school day. Until she got to speak with him she needed to be strong for Violet, even though she felt far from strong herself and the now uncontrollable shiver was making her bones feel like they were rattling apart under her skin.

At midday, the blinds to the apothecary shop remained drawn and a tomb-like quietness had settled over Cupola House. Nancy and Violet sat at the kitchen table. Nancy's breakfast crumpet was untouched and her sister's was only half eaten.

Violet's cheeks were tear-stained. "I want Mother," she sniffed. "And Father. I want him too. I don't want to stay in this silly old house. I want to go home."

Home. They had only been away for four days, but it suddenly seemed so very far away. Nancy wished she could view their home through the telescope in the cupola, across the fields and rivers and valleys, past the industrial mills and canals until she could see their town house with its familiar yellow curtains, the scent of wood polish and Monty the dog.

There was a gentle *rap, rap, rap* at the back door. Nancy looked up and saw a reedy figure behind the obscured glass. *Burch.* She pushed her chair back, knocking it over with a thump in her hurry. Unlocking the door, she swung it open. "You're not at school?" she cried.

"It's lunchtime and I snuck out. Has your ma been arrested? For that's what I heard said in the schoolyard."

Nancy nodded, a rush of angry tears filling her eyes. She blinked them back. She would not cry, not in front of Violet or her new friend.

"I don't believe it," said Burch, giving Nancy a firm look. "Why would she try to burn down the mayor's house?" He came in and sat at the kitchen table next to Violet. His slender fingers drummed on the wood.

Nancy shook her head. "She didn't," she said, locking the door and slumping into a seat opposite them. "Mother said it was a case of mistaken identity, but how can that be?"

"Mother doesn't like the mayor one small bit," said Violet slowly. She threw them a nervous look and chewed on her already ragged thumbnail.

The clatter of a handcart being pushed along the street cobbles above rumbled into the kitchen. A wood pigeon cooed on a nearby chimney pot.

"What do you mean?" asked Nancy, leaning forward.

Tears filled Violet's eyes.

"Anything you know that could help your ma is a good thing," said Burch kindly.

"Mother said...she said..." Violet stuttered.

"Come on," said Burch, giving her an encouraging smile.

"It was when we played hide-and-seek," Violet said, looking at Nancy.

Nancy nodded. "I found you in the cupola."

Violet rubbed her pink nose and sniffed. "At first I hid behind the curtains on the landing near Mother's bedroom. She came out of her room and was talking to herself...she said...she said she wished the mayor had never graced this earth. Doesn't that mean she wished he was...dead?"

Nancy sat back in her chair, a sliver of cold arching up her back. This must explain why Violet had been behaving oddly the past few days whenever the mayor was mentioned.

"Do you think Mother did try to burn the mayor's house down?" asked Violet in a small voice. "They found one of her handkerchiefs."

Nancy shook her head, while wondering if she really *could* have done such a thing. The police said there was a witness. Mother had admitted to being at the mayor's house last night. Had she gone there to burn his house down? If found guilty, she would certainly go to prison. Nancy remembered her father once telling her of a man who had accidentally set fire to a pile of expensive wood belonging to his employer. He was sent to prison for three years. Bitterness rose in her throat. They had to act quickly to find some proof that their mother was not to blame. There was only one thing to do – visit the police station, try and find out who their witness was and discover exactly what was going to happen to Mother next.

CHAPTER 22

The Witness

While washing up their dirty plates, Nancy told Burch and Violet about her plan to go to the police station. Burch's eyes widened, but he gave her a quick nod.

Violet looked a little happier. "Maybe the police will let us see Mother?"

But something occurred to Nancy. "No. We can't tell the policemen who we are. There must be a very good reason Mother said we should not talk to strangers. I think she was trying to keep us hidden from the mayor. He must not know Mr Greenstone is our grandfather."

Violet nodded solemnly. Nancy took her upstairs to get dressed, then made an additional trip up to the third floor to listen at her grandfather's door. It was quiet inside his room and she knocked gently. "Grandfather? Are you all right?"

"Yes, dear," Grandfather replied weakly. "I shall be downstairs as soon my head is less muddled."

"But Mother didn't do it, did she?" asked Nancy. A flat silence followed which dried out her mouth.

"No. She did not," said her grandfather eventually.

"But surely there is some evidence that proves that?" said Nancy.

"I don't know, dear girl. I just don't know," was her grandfather's reply. She waited for a few minutes more, hoping he might say something else, but the ear she pressed to the door heard only the regular creaks of the floorboards as he paced around the room.

Back in the kitchen Nancy scribbled a quick note to their grandfather telling him they had gone for a walk, just in case he decided to emerge from his room while they were gone. He had told them to stay inside and keep the door locked, but she felt sure that following his instructions was not the right thing to do. She had done her best to unlock the secrets her mother was keeping but had failed. With Mother gone she had to take more direct action, whatever the consequences. She bustled Violet into her cardigan and Burch gave her a questioning look. "I can't leave her here," she whispered, giving her friend a shrug.

"We'll leave her with my ma at the haberdashery," said Burch. "Police stations are no places for little-uns."

"But I want to come with you," protested Violet.

"Please, Violet. We shan't be long. I promise to tell you everything I learn from the police," said Nancy.

Violet did up her cardigan buttons silently. Nancy stepped forward and hugged her sister. "There is no need to worry, everything will get sorted out," she whispered in her ear.

Violet looked up, her eyes teary. "But how can it get sorted out with Mother gone and Father in Leeds and Grandfather upstairs in his room?" she sniffed.

"It will get sorted out because Burch and I are here. Horrid things have been happening, but we will do our best to get to the bottom of them and make things better," said Nancy, hoping that her words were true.

184

The three children walked into the haberdashery shop to find Mrs Cavendish serving a dark-haired lady who was examining the embroidery silks. "This is a strong thread, Mrs Gilbert. Perfect for tapestry work." Mrs Cavendish looked up. "Burch, shouldn't you be in school? Oh, hello, girls. How nice to see you again."

"There's something I must help Nancy with – an errand she has to run. Would you be able to watch Violet for a while, please, Ma?" asked Burch.

"This errand must be important, for it is unlike you to miss school out of choice," said Mrs Cavendish with a frown.

"It is important," said Burch.

"And I suppose you can't tell me why?" asked Mrs Cavendish, not unkindly.

Nancy wished they could tell Mrs Cavendish their troubles, but as his ma did not agree with Burch making deliveries to their grandfather's shop, she felt they were unlikely to get any sympathy or help from her if she knew the truth.

Mrs Gilbert smiled at Nancy. "Children will have their secrets, Mrs Cavendish. I would not worry. Have you been up late watching the comet, girls? It's quite a spectacle, isn't it? My Alfred and I work in a kitchen garden and we stand near the hothouses each night as it streaks across the sky. It's tremendous."

"It is," replied Nancy, watching Burch head towards the door.

Mrs Gilbert glanced at Violet, who was standing pale-faced beside Mrs Cavendish. "I have a niece about your sister's age," she said to Nancy. "Clara, her name is. Alfred and I hope to visit her and her older brother Christopher soon – that's if the earl can spare us from the house and gardens. We're busy getting produce ready for the mayor's comet party tomorrow – including three home-grown pineapples. The earl is always happy to support a worthy cause." She fiddled with a gold cross hanging on a delicate chain round her neck.

"Come on, Nancy. We should be going," said Burch, who was waiting by the door.

"Bye, Violet. I promise I won't be long," said Nancy. Violet gave Nancy a small nod. Nancy felt a curl of worry for her sister – it was just the two of them now and she needed to look after Violet and keep her safe, but the best way she could do that was to find out what had happened to their mother and get her home.

Burch led the way to the police station, his long strides meaning Nancy was always a few steps behind. The more Nancy thought of the morning's events, the more outrageous things seemed. Her mother arrested for arson. A sudden image of Father's battered brown briefcase leaning against the coat stand at home sprang into her head. It was where he kept his cardboard files of notes on the cases he was involved with. Each folder had a name on the front. *Arthur Jones. Sarah Belstead.* Those people had been arrested for crimes and were facing prison. Would her own mother now have a file with *her* name on it? A burst of fear made her hands tremble and she pushed them into her pockets.

Burch waited for Nancy to catch up as they walked past an imposing building with six stone columns supporting carvings of corn sheaves and sheep. "I reckon this will all be sorted out in a jiffy. It must be a misunderstanding."

Nancy grimaced as they continued onward through the market square, where carriages and motor cars waited, the smells of hot leather horse harnesses and exhaust fumes mingling. Beyond the square, the skyline was peppered with a few industrial chimney stacks and large gas storage cylinders. They passed small children with dusty faces playing in the street with a hoop and ball, heard a baby crying from an upstairs window, and saw mothers chatting on doorsteps. These people were having just another normal day at home. The thought of her own home brought a sudden clench of longing, but also a fresh resolve that she would do whatever she could to help her mother.

As they approached the red-brick police station, Nancy pushed her heels into the pavement and hurried forward. She walked through its wooden door, Burch following close behind.

The reception area was small and wood-panelled, with four bench seats under a high window. There was a wall of obscured glass behind the counter, in front of which a uniformed man with bushy eyebrows sat at a desk. "Yes?" he sighed. "What is it? Stolen bicycle?" He tilted his head in a bored manner, then his eyebrows lifted as he looked at Burch. "Oh. Morning, Burch. What brings you here…with this young lady?"

Nancy felt the hairs on her arms prickle. She had felt brave walking to the police station, but now they had arrived all of that courage had tumbled out of her.

"Morning, Constable Addison," said Burch. He

glanced at Nancy. "We've come to ask about an arrest made this morning."

The constable leaned forward on the desk, looking slightly more interested than before. "Have you now? May I ask why?" He was looking Nancy up and down, as if assessing her standing in society. Were her shoes polished, her clothes neat and tidy?

"Charlotte…Greenstone. She's been wrongly arrested for a crime against…the mayor," Nancy said hesitantly, her tongue stumbling over the use of her mother's maiden name.

Constable Addison picked up his pencil and tapped it on his chin thoughtfully. "Wrongly arrested? Why would you say that, Miss?"

"I know of the Greenstone family," Nancy said, hoping she was not giving too much away. "I believe… Miss Greenstone is a churchgoer and a member of the Women's Institute and last year won the prize for best…stitched handkerchief." Burch nudged her in the side. "And she was also runner-up in the Victoria sponge competition," she blurted out in a rush, wiping her sweaty palms on her skirts.

A small smile crinkled the skin around Constable Addison's eyes. "Best Victoria sponge? Well, that is quite an accolade. And how exactly do you know Miss Greenstone, may I ask?"

Nancy felt the constable's eyes boring into her, seeking out the truth. He would be disappointed, for she was not going to give it. "Miss Greenstone is…a family friend," she said.

"All we want to know is what'll happen to Miss Greenstone now she's been arrested? And we wanted to ask about the witness to the crime," said Burch quickly.

The constable turned his attention to Burch. "Have you been speaking to your pa? Is that why you're here. He's not supposed to speak of this."

Nancy glanced at Burch, her jaw dropping.

"My pa saw Miss Greenstone commit arson? He is the witness?" whispered Burch, the colour leaching from his cheeks.

Constable Addison glanced behind him, to the obscured glass. He turned back. "I am sorry, Burch. I'm not permitted to speak of it."

Burch gave Nancy an anxious look. She stared back at him, unsure where to put her thoughts. Burch and his father *had* bumped into each other on the street last night when he had been following her mother and grandfather. Mr Cavendish could have witnessed the attempted arson if he had been passing the mayor's house at that time.

"Is Miss Greenstone here, at this police station?" asked Nancy, feeling quite breathless. "Is she allowed visitors?" The image of her mother's dressing gown billowing from under her coat would not leave her head. Had she been given some clothes to wear?

The constable's eyebrows lifted into his hairline. "This crime is a serious one. At Mayor Douglas's request, Miss Greenstone has been taken to the prison to await her trial."

A wave of dizziness washed over Nancy. *The prison.*

The children walked out of the police station into the brightness of the day in silence. Burch leaned against the wall of the building, and rubbed the back of his neck.

"She didn't do it," said Nancy quietly. "She can't have done." Lack of sleep and worry were making her feel unmoored, as if she was watching these events happen to someone else. She placed a hand on the wall, trying to ground herself.

Burch didn't reply. He just rubbed his neck some more, then pulled his hands away and shoved them into his trouser pockets.

"If only I could get a message to my mother, or talk to her. I am sure I could find out the truth. I'm not saying your father is lying, but he must be mistaken about who he saw last night," Nancy continued.

A heavy silence settled over them.

Burch suddenly straightened his shoulders and began to walk back towards the market square.

"Hey, where are you going?" Nancy cried.

Burch gestured for her to follow. "I make deliveries," he said.

"So?" said Nancy, staring at him.

"I make deliveries all over town, including where your mother is right now," Burch said.

"Oh! He makes deliveries to the prison," Nancy murmured to herself. "Wait," she said, running to catch him up. "Making deliveries is one thing, but getting a message to a prisoner being held there is surely another?"

"I know people who work there, and it's got to be worth a try," said Burch, his jaw set firm. "I can't say what my pa did or didn't see, but you need to keep believing that your ma is innocent."

Nancy felt a tremor in her breastbone and blinked away the tears threatening to fall. She gave Burch a shaky smile and nodded. He was right. She badly needed help and she was prepared to put all of her trust in her friend. There was no one else who could help her, after all.

CHAPTER 23

Photograph

Nancy's eyes followed the length of the crenellated prison wall. The place had an air of coldness and despair about it. What was her mother doing in there? Was she warm? Did she have enough to eat?

Burch led them past the large wooden doors Nancy had seen through the telescope, then took a left turn, continuing down a narrow lane alongside the prison wall. A short way down, Burch stopped in front of a black door with a hinged window flap set behind iron bars. He yanked on the bell pull and Nancy heard a distant clang marking their arrival.

A minute or so later the window flap opened inwards and a woman peeped through the bars. "Oh hello, Burch. I wasn't expecting you until tomorrow with the meat delivery. Give me a minute and I'll open up." There was the grumble of keys being turned and bolts drawn back. The door opened and the woman wiped her hands on an apron smeared with blood-red streaks. She saw Nancy looking at it and let out a crackly laugh. "Been boiling up tripe for the prisoners' tea."

Nancy felt a wave of nausea. Mother hated tripe. She said even the thought of it made her feel ill.

"I've a favour to ask, Eliza," said Burch.

"A favour? Of course, my love. Anything for my favourite godson. You always bring me the best from the butcher's and fishmonger's."

Nancy blinked. *Burch was Eliza's godson?*

Burch cleared his throat. "My friend here needs to get a message to a prisoner…and one back out again. Can you help us?"

Eliza's face creased into a heavy frown. She stepped out of the doorway and looked up and down the lane. "Get a message to one of the prisoners?" she hissed. "Burch, have you lost your marbles?"

"Um, no. I don't reckon so," replied Burch calmly.

Eliza laughed shrilly and shook her head.

"Please, Eliza," said Burch, stepping forward. "It's urgent."

Eliza opened her mouth to speak and then closed it again. She shook her head. "Impossible at the moment," she muttered. "I'd lose my position if I got found out – or worse. I prepare the food for those prisoners and, believe me, I've no intention of eating it myself."

"Please," said Nancy quietly. "A person in there did not commit the crime she was accused of and I need to find out what happened."

"What's she accused of then?" asked Eliza.

"Arson," said Nancy quietly, horrified that this word was in any way connected with her mother.

"'Tis a serious crime, arson," Eliza said, her eyes widening. She turned and pulled Burch by the collar. "Now you listen here, young Burch. Since the comet stirred everything up and got people on edge, wardens are patrolling all hours of the day and night and it's impossible to smuggle items in for the prisoners."

"Please help us," said Nancy, feeling a little more hopeful, as it seemed prisoners *had* received items from outside the walls before.

"Eliza! What's keeping you?" called a voice from inside.

Eliza pressed her fingers to her temples and sighed. "You be back here at eleven o'clock tonight with your correspondence. And I'll be expecting a side of good mutton from you tomorrow," she said, with a jab at Burch's chest – but her eyes had a softness about them.

Nancy's stomach unwound a little. "Thank you," she said.

"Don't thank me yet," Eliza replied. "What's this woman's name?"

"Mrs Rivers…but when they arrested her the policeman called her Miss Charlotte Greenstone," said Nancy.

Eliza gave her a pitying look. "Your friend is a *Greenstone*?"

Nancy nodded as she held her breath. Perhaps Eliza knew of her grandfather's poor reputation in the town and would refuse to help.

"Eliza, will you come back here now! The tripe's boiling dry," cried a voice from inside.

"Eleven o'clock tonight – don't be late," Eliza whispered, turning quickly and shutting the door in their faces.

As Nancy and Burch walked away from the prison and back towards the town, Nancy saw the cupola and one of its small arched windows rising above all the other rooftops. It was the highest point for miles around and made Nancy think of the golden eagles she had learned about at school, choosing the tallest and best trees for their nests. It also provided a direct view of the prison. If her mother and grandfather had been watching and visiting the prison, was it just coincidence that her mother was now locked up in there too? These thoughts made her head ache. Even if she could get a message to her mother, all kinds of things might go wrong. Perhaps the time had come to seek help from elsewhere after all. "I think I need to speak with my father and ask for his help," said Nancy miserably.

"It will be a shock for him to learn what's happened, that's for sure," said Burch. "You could wait until tomorrow, see if you get a message from your ma first. Then you'd have something concrete to tell your pa at least."

Burch was right, it would be a shock. A terrible one. Nancy imagined her father's kind eyes narrowing with horror, his voice rising in alarm.

Burch came to a sudden stop. He looked down a

narrow cut that led through to another street. "The mayor's house is down there."

Nancy peered towards the street. An image of her mother pushing a smouldering handkerchief through the mayor's letter box and Burch's father there to witness it flew into her head. She had a sudden urge to trace her mother's footsteps from last night, place herself in her mother's shoes and see what Burch's father had seen. Nancy's jaw clenched and she set off along the cut, Burch following close behind.

"Are you sure this is a good idea, Nancy?" Burch said, his voice threaded with anxiety.

"I just want to understand what your father saw for myself," Nancy replied. "Don't you think it's odd that he's been having all of this trouble with the mayor and he is the only witness?"

Burch's eyebrows tugged together and he was quiet as they continued to walk. They emerged onto a long street of higgledy-piggledy pastel-pink, ochre and white terraced houses. Burch pointed to the house on the corner. "That's his – the white timber-framed one."

It was a small property, the leaded windows so old they were leaning outwards. The house was pretty but unremarkable. Nancy imagined Mayor Douglas might have lived somewhere far grander with lush green lawns leading up to a house with pillars and diamond-paned windows. She noticed that his front door was blackened around the letter box, the paint peeling and blistered. *Surely her mother could not have pushed a burning handkerchief through this letter box?* There was not as much visible damage as she had imagined – at least the fire had been caught before it had taken hold; the mayor's property had been saved.

As Nancy's eyes remained fixed on the door, she thought about the mayor saying her mother had got what she deserved. Was her mother seeking revenge for something the mayor had done? The thought sickened Nancy and, try as she might, she could not accept the police's conclusion. "I don't believe my mother started the fire, but I think the mayor has a strong reason for accusing her of it," she said with renewed conviction.

Burch scratched his nose as he gave her a sidelong glance. "But why would my pa lie about seeing your ma start the fire?"

"Do *you* think your father would lie?" asked Nancy.

"He's always been an honest man, never been in trouble with the law. Perhaps he just made a mistake?" said Burch, his voice edged with hope.

Nancy didn't want to believe Mr Cavendish was capable of lying either, but the mayor clearly had a hold over him. Could Mayor Douglas have persuaded Burch's father to be a false witness? That was a serious crime in itself and she could not think why Burch's father would ever agree to such a terrible request. And how would the mayor have come to have one of her mother's handkerchiefs? Solving this mystery was like trying to poke a piece of thread through the eye of a very small needle – it required a good eye and concentration, both of which she felt she was lacking at that moment. But while they were here, perhaps there was something else they could do that might be useful. "Come on," said Nancy, pulling Burch across the road.

"What are you doing?" he said, striding to keep up with her.

"The mayor's red motor car isn't parked outside. He must be out," Nancy said.

"He might still be at home. Sometimes Pa takes the motor car out to refuel it," said Burch anxiously.

But Nancy had already walked to the side of the mayor's house and, glancing quickly up and down the quiet street to ensure she wasn't being watched, she leaned in to look through a downstairs window.

She cupped her hands to her eyes to reduce the glare of the sun.

The drawing room was just as she would have imagined a mayor's house to look: plush velvet chairs, thick rugs and fat silver candlesticks above the fireplace. Next to the window there was a well-stocked drinks cabinet, and on it a single sepia photograph in a gilded frame. Nancy blinked.

The photograph was of Cupola House.

Outside it stood two people; a young man and a woman wearing a wide-brimmed hat. They were arm in arm. The man was unmistakable – it was the mayor, although he was somewhat younger. The woman's dark hair and eyes seemed familiar too. She looked a little like her mother. But it couldn't be, could it? "Look, Burch," she said, reaching behind to tug on her friend's sleeve. "What do you think of this…?" But her fingers grasped at thin air.

She turned to see that Burch was a few paces behind and staring up at the first-floor window, his jaw slack. "We need to go, now," he whispered.

Nancy stepped back and slowly looked up, her eyes settling on pale-as-pearl cheeks and dark eyes. The mayor! His gaze was piercing, but he seemed more interested than cross to find them looking through his window. He placed a palm to the glass and peered at them more closely.

"We need to run," said Burch in a low voice. And they did, Nancy glancing back one final time only to see the blank eyes of the mayor's windows watching them as they fled down the street.

Chapter 24

Message to Mother

After collecting Violet from the haberdashery, Nancy dashed back to Cupola House, fielding her sister's questions as best she could, thinking of everything that had happened all the while.

"Did you see Mother?"

"Why not?"

"When can we see her?"

"When will she be home, Nancy?"

"I miss her."

"I wish Father was here."

"If things aren't sorted out by tomorrow, I promise

I will find a way to telephone Father at his office," said Nancy, and Violet seemed a little soothed by this. Arriving back at the house they found the apothecary shop shut, the blinds drawn. Grandfather must still be thinking in his room. How could they tempt him out?

The sausages and boiled potatoes which Nancy cooked and left outside his bedroom door for lunch remained untouched.

The book on herbal remedies Violet selected from the library to read to him seemed to go unheard.

Telling him that the plants on the landing were a little dry and needed his care and attention did nothing to rouse him from his stupor.

What were they to do about Grandfather? Nancy had been thrust into the role of a grown-up and she didn't like it. But there was no time to waste and if taking on adult responsibilities was what it took to save Mother, then she would just grit her teeth and get on with it.

Nancy eventually got Violet ready for bed, tucking her up and kissing her on her forehead, in the same way that Mother and Father did every evening. "You're being very brave."

Violet rubbed her eyes and smiled. "Will you stay with me for a while?"

"Of course," said Nancy, her chest expanding with love and worry for her little sister. She lay down beside Violet and curled up against her back, feeling the soft tickle of her hair against her cheek. With a pinch of longing she could almost imagine they were back in the bedroom they had shared in Leeds, with its pink striped wallpaper and shelf of stuffed bears, board games and books in the corner.

As soon as she heard her sister's soft snores, Nancy got up and crept down to the kitchen. She could not stop thinking about the photograph she had seen in the mayor's house, and the interested look the mayor had given her as he watched from the window. A shiver crossed Nancy's shoulders as she realized he must have recognized her from the haberdashery shop. She pushed the worrying thought away, sat at the table and pondered over what she should write in the message she hoped would reach her mother in prison. Flattening the piece of paper, Nancy picked up a pencil and began to write.

Dearest Mother,
I am certain you did not commit arson. Burch (my new friend) and I want to prove you are innocent, but you need to be truthful with us.

Is the mayor accusing you of starting the fire as revenge for something that happened in the past? I don't care how dreadful the truth is, you <u>must</u> tell me all of it. Please try and reply (I believe someone will help smuggle your message out to me) so I can tell Father and get his help.

Fondest love, Nancy

P.S. We both miss you and are well. I hope prison isn't too dreadful and you've avoided the tripe.

Nancy knew that if this letter got into the wrong hands, it could make life far worse for her mother, and for her. But it was a risk that needed to be taken.

As they had agreed, at quarter to eleven that night, Burch tapped on the back door. Nancy sprang to her feet and opened it. He didn't say a word, just gestured for Nancy to follow.

Putting on her coat and locking the door behind her, they walked briskly through the quiet streets, keeping away from the street lamps and to the shadows. Nancy breathed in the thin night air, her eyes drawn upwards. The comet's tail was flaring across the sky. People were standing on their doorsteps watching the night as they walked past.

As they drew closer to the prison Nancy's jaw clenched until her teeth ached. She thought about the mayor's party to celebrate the comet arriving at its closest point to Earth the next night, Burch's father's help in preparing for it and him being witness to her mother's supposed crime. She felt these things were connected, but how? Something swooped and flitted in the air above Nancy's head and she looked up.

"It's just a flittermouse," said Burch, looking up too. "A bat off to the water meadows to hunt for midges and moths."

"A flittermouse?" whispered Nancy.

Burch smiled, his teeth shining. "I'm guessing they're not called that in Leeds?"

"No, but I like your word for them much better," said Nancy, thankful for a moment of distraction from her thoughts.

The prison loomed into view, the high walls of the yard reaching upwards into the night. Nancy's right eyelid twitched. Would Eliza be able to deliver the letter? Would she and Burch be seen outside if they waited for a reply?

"If things go wrong and the message falls into the wrong hands, we'll tell them it was my idea, that you wanted no part of this," whispered Burch, as they arrived at the door.

The words glowed like a lantern in Nancy's chest. Burch barely knew her and yet he was prepared to take the blame and all the punishments that would go with it. She stood taller and flashed him a smile. "It won't go wrong," she whispered. "But thank you anyway."

He returned the smile, his eyes glittering like brass buttons.

The sound of the bolts and locks being pulled back disturbed the stillness of the night. The door opened a crack and an arm wound round it, fingers urgently beckoning them forward. Nancy took the message from her pocket with trembling fingers, ready to push it into Eliza's hand. But instead the fingers curled round Nancy's coat sleeve and yanked her through the door. Nancy swallowed a yelp as she stumbled into a dark hallway and the heavy wooden door slammed behind her with a thump.

CHAPTER 25

Inside

Nancy's chest tightened as her eyes adjusted to the dimly lit passageway. A prison guard, not much taller than she was, stood in front of her, the creases on the sleeves of his blue uniform as sharp as knives. "Follow my instructions. Don't speak. Tread softly. Keep your head down. Understand?" he whispered.

Nancy's legs wobbled. "Where is Eliza?" she whispered. "I was expecting to…"

"Quiet," whispered the guard. "Eliza has asked me to deal with this. Greenstone – is that who you want to see?"

"Um…I have a message for her," squeaked Nancy, holding it out to him. "I really shouldn't be in here…"

The guard gave her a disapproving tut. "I said no speaking."

Nancy pressed her lips together and gave him a quick nod, her stomach somersaulting in sickening loops.

"You'll have five minutes with her. When you hear a knock on the cell door, you come out immediately. Understood?"

Nancy felt the hairs lift on the nape of her neck. *This guard was taking her to see her mother?* But she was twelve. She had no business being inside a prison. What must Burch be thinking as he waited for her? This was not the plan – he would be frantic.

The guard turned and began to walk down the long passageway. Nancy glanced behind to the locked door leading back outside. As frightening as this was, she longed to see her mother and make sure she was all right. Making a quick decision she followed the guard, the smells of overcooked meat and stewed vegetables seeping beneath a series of half-open doors.

At the end of the passage the guard pulled a large bronze key from the ring attached to his belt and unlocked another door. He then selected a smaller key, bent down and turned it in a second lock at the bottom, and did the same again with a third lock at the top of the door.

Nancy had never seen the outside of a prison before but had listened keenly to her father when he told of visiting his clients in Armley Gaol in Leeds. His jaw would be set firm, his eyes sorrowful. "Prisons are the darkest of places, my dear," he would say. "Those who have made grave errors are locked away in conditions that still require much improving." Her father was part of a group campaigning for prison reforms, to ensure better conditions for prisoners, but he would only give her the scarcest of details. Nancy wished she had pursued her questioning about prisons further, for it might have squashed some of the fear she was feeling now.

The prison guard saw Nancy looking at the keys and bolts. "Can never be too careful," he muttered. "Three keys mean fewer escapees, is the motto here."

Nancy wiped her clammy hands on her coat, opened her mouth to question him further on this, then closed it again when he placed a finger to his lips. "Now, wait on the other side of the door. Fred will come for you. Do exactly as he says."

Nancy's insides dropped again. *Who was Fred?* She opened her mouth to protest, but before she could get the words out, the guard pushed her through the door, closed it behind her and she heard the sound of the three locks being secured.

Standing with her back to the door, Nancy squeezed her hands into fists and tried to slow her rapid breaths. She was outside in the fresh air again, on the perimeter of a large, enclosed yard. She looked up and saw the brilliance of the comet above. It was even brighter than earlier and it calmed her a little. She needed to remember that her fear and this unexpected situation would pass, for better or worse, just like the comet.

She glanced around. The yard was empty. How long would she have to wait for Fred – whoever he was? She dragged in a deep and steadying breath. She was suddenly distracted by a noise to her right. A rather strange clucking noise that most certainly did not belong in a prison yard. *Chickens.* They must have been disturbed by her unexpected entrance.

"Shush," she whispered desperately, as the clucking grew ever noisier, now accompanied by pecking and scuffling. She looked at the birds' dim, scrawny bodies as they busied about in their wire pen. "Shush," she whispered again, but the clucking grew louder still.

With a rising horror, Nancy saw a light flick on across the yard and a curtain pull back. Was that where the governor lived? Her father had told her stories about prison governors, how they ran their institutions with a rod of iron. She ran over to the chickens who were bustling about in their pen as if a fox was on the prowl. "Shush, shush," she begged one particularly vocal bird. Her grandfather in York kept chickens at the bottom of his garden. Sometimes when they fussed it helped to pick them up. She bent down, grabbed the noisy bird and held it close to her chest, its wings flapping in protest then quietening. She leaned back against the wall, her knees weak with relief.

"Hey, who's that hiding over there?" called a low voice.

Nancy felt a fresh tremble of terror. Another man in a guard's uniform emerged from the shadows and was striding towards her across the yard with a flashlight. Was this Fred? He did not look as if he had been expecting her. A giant lump in her throat prevented her from swallowing. The chicken continued to cluck softly in her arms, as light dazzled her eyes and the sound of the guard's heavy footsteps thudded towards her. How could she possibly explain her presence here? If she were to be found with the message to her mother in her pocket, would they lock her up too?

CHAPTER 26

Delivery

Nancy's heart clattered against her ribs as the chicken wriggled and clucked under her arm.

"You're just a girl," said the prison guard in surprise. "And whatever are you doing with Doreen the chicken?" The guard lowered his flashlight and Nancy blinked. This guard was taller than the one who had let her into the yard, a cotton-wool-like beard half obscuring his face. The remaining chickens in the pen clucked. He turned to them. "Hush, Isobel. Hush, Winnie. You should be sleeping, saving your energy for egg laying."

The chickens shuffled and began to quieten. Pushing

the flashlight into his pocket, the guard stepped forward, gently taking Doreen from Nancy and returning her to the wire pen, where she flapped her wings and began to settle. He then turned back to face Nancy. "How did you get in here? You don't look much older than my Sally, and she's just turned ten."

"Actually, I'll be thirteen next birthday," said Nancy tremulously, rather offended that he thought her so young. She stood a little taller and straightened her shoulders.

The guard peered into the darkness of the yard. "Are there others with you? Did you climb the wall?"

"Um…no," said Nancy.

"Well how do you explain yourself then?" asked the guard, plonking his hands on his hips. "This is a prison, not a place you can just wander into. Is this a prank of some sort? Has someone helped you get inside?"

Nancy pushed her shaking hands into her coat pockets. If she told the guard about Burch, Eliza, and the guard who had got her here, they would be in tremendous trouble. She would have to try and sort out this problem on her own.

"You'd better come with me," the guard said, placing a hand on her arm.

"Please...please don't lock me up," whispered Nancy. "I have a little sister and..."

"Lock you up, why ever would I do that?" he interrupted. "Unless you've done something that deserves a locking up."

Nancy shook her head violently. What should she say to this man? Where was he going to take her – to see the governor?

"Come on, little girls like you don't belong in a place like this," the guard said, leading her across the yard.

Nancy swallowed the dryness from her mouth as they passed a row of planting beds, the vegetable tops waving eerily in the breeze.

"Nice view of the comet tonight," the guard said, tipping his head to the sky, then giving Nancy a quick glance. "Not that it's a good thing, mind. Caused a lot of unrest here – had riots the other week."

Nancy sensed he was trying to reassure her, but this talk of unrest and riots was actually making her even more apprehensive. "Is it...safe out here?" she asked.

"Safe enough," he said. "Some prisoners are certain we're doomed because of the gas from the comet's tail – they won't listen to those that say otherwise. We've had to take away prisoners' privileges and invoke a curfew, lock them all in their cells until the comet has passed."

"All of them?" asked Nancy quietly, thinking of her poor mother locked up and all alone. Melancholy weighed heavy on her shoulders. She supposed this guard was either taking her to the governor or showing her to the main gate, which meant no message delivery and no visit to Mother.

The guard suddenly stopped and turned to face Nancy. Glancing around, he pulled her towards the darkness of the perimeter wall. "Are you here to see someone, Miss? I've taken over Fred's yard duties tonight because he's unwell. Was he going to help you?"

"Um. Yes. It's n...not what I was expecting to happen, though," stammered Nancy. The guard was giving her an encouraging look. She reached into her pocket for the message to her mother. It would be a risk, but one she had to take. Pulling out the piece of paper she held it out to the guard. "But I did want to get a message to someone," she said quickly.

The guard gave her a brief nod, his beard jiggling. "Who?"

"Her name is…Greenstone," said Nancy.

"Greenstone," the guard mumbled. "She's been here a while."

"Since yesterday," said Nancy with a frown.

The guard gave her an odd look. "Come on. Best be quick then."

"You'll take the message to her?" Nancy asked, her lungs expanding with hope.

"I can do better than that. You can see her, but you'll only have a few minutes, then I'm taking you out. The governor sometimes does night patrols and if he caught you in here, it would not be good for either of us. Fred and I deliver packages to the prisoners on occasion, things from their families. Greenstone is one we've delivered to in the past, but deliveries have had to stop since the unrest – too risky."

Nancy shook her head in confusion. "But she's only been locked up since…'

"Come on," urged the guard, gesturing for her to follow him. "And please do be quiet." He led Nancy across the yard, unlocked another door and gently pushed her inside. As they traipsed quietly up a flight of stone stairs, Nancy pressed her arms into her sides and tried to ignore the bars on the windows, the smell of damp and mould radiating from the cold floor. Then they were standing in a long corridor of blue doors with barred peepholes. Nancy shivered, heard the slow *drip, drip, drip* of water. What were the stories of the people behind these doors? How had they ended up in this awful place? She suddenly felt quite jittery at the thought of her mother's arms around her again, hardly believing that luck was on her side and the guard she had feared was actually prepared to help.

The guard took a key from the huge ring attached to his belt, unlocked the cell door and swung it open a fraction. "In you go then. Five minutes and I'll be back. And remember – no raised voices," he whispered.

Nancy nodded, every muscle in her body tightening in fear and anticipation. Stepping inside, she felt the draught of the door being closed and heard the clunk of the heavy key turning. A small barred window high on the wall threw a square of pearlescent light into the small cell. Her mother was half sitting up in a bed under the window, rubbing her eyes.

"Mother?" whispered Nancy tentatively, taking a step forward. "It's me." The words hung in the dark like a spider's web.

Her mother flung back the bedcovers and in three

steps was on the other side of the room standing in front of Nancy.

Nancy stared at her short dark hair. Short dark hair? Her mother had dark hair, but it wasn't short. She also did not have such a thin and wavering frame. With a jolt of horror, Nancy realized that the person standing in front of her was not her mother at all.

CHAPTER 27

Cell

"Who...who are you?" whispered Nancy, stepping backwards until she bumped into the cell door.

"I might ask you the same thing," whispered the woman hoarsely. Her arms hung limply at the sides of her plain nightgown, which even in the dull light Nancy saw was grey and worn.

"I thought...I expected...I was supposed to be seeing my...mother," Nancy stammered, unable to keep a choke from her voice. She slipped her trembling fingers into her coat pockets and balled them into fists.

"But…you're just a girl," said the woman, her face softening a little. "Did Callum bring you in? He sometimes smuggles in letters and parcels for the prisoners but hasn't been able to for a while because of the comet. Although, you are slightly larger than the average parcel. Who *is* your mother, perhaps I know of her?"

"Charlotte Rivers…I mean Greenstone. I'm Nancy, her daughter. Do you know her?" Nancy said, thinking that this situation required absolute honesty.

The woman stilled, as if an icy blast of arctic wind had rushed in from the window and frozen her solid. "Greenstone?" she whispered incredulously. "Your mother's name was Greenstone? And you are Nancy?"

"Yes," whispered Nancy, blinking back tears, as everything else poured out. "She's been arrested for arson against the mayor and locked up, but I know she didn't do it. The guard was going to give me five minutes with her – I have a message."

The woman swayed and grabbed at the wall to steady herself. She let out a low moan, like an animal, and pressed a hand to her cheek. "Charlotte. Charlotte came back. Why did she come back?"

Nancy's brain swam in confusion.

The woman dropped her hands. She took a step forward.

Nancy clutched at the door she was leaning against, more afraid than ever.

The woman lifted a hand and Nancy winced, thinking the prisoner might be about to strike her, but instead she reached for a strand of Nancy's hair and let it run through her fingers like sand. A bolt of cold made Nancy shiver and jerk away from her touch.

"Don't be afraid, my dear Nancy. I am Agatha, your mother's sister," said the woman.

Nancy blinked. Blinked again.

"Callum brought you to the wrong Greenstone," Agatha whispered, shaking her head. She suddenly reached for Nancy's icy hands, led her to the bed and sat her down.

Nancy felt light as a feather, as if she were floating. "You are my aunt?" she said, staring at Agatha. She glanced down at Agatha's fingers, which were still wound around hers. Agatha's nails were square, just like her mother's and her own. Agatha had a similar nose to hers and her mother's; a slight kink to the right. "But Mother never said a word about having a sister," she said, thoughts about the mother she knew rearranging yet again.

Agatha glanced at the cell door. "Tell me exactly what happened – you say she is accused of arson against the mayor, against Percival?"

Nancy nodded, tears rushing to her eyes.

Agatha gave her a piercing look. "My husband is not to be trusted."

A tsunami of dizziness washed over Nancy. *Agatha was married to the beastly mayor?* Agatha gently let go of Nancy's hands, picked up a square cloth from a small table next to her bed and passed it to her niece. *A handkerchief edged in red ribbon.*

Nancy blinked. "This handkerchief – where did it come from?"

"Your mother sews them and sends them to me so I can signal to my father. Often they get confiscated, so she sends more via one of the guards," said Agatha.

A burst of understanding hit Nancy, parts of the puzzle finally slotting into place. She stroked the red-ribboned edging. "You take these handkerchiefs into the prison yard and wave them. Grandfather sees you from the telescope in the cupola."

Agatha nodded. "It's been our signal for years now, a small comfort for him and for me. But since the unrest about the comet I have been locked in my cell, unable to make contact." Her voice trailed off.

The whispered conversations Nancy had overheard between her mother and grandfather, and their reason for coming here, were finally making sense. The small packages her mother and grandfather had been delivering must have been handkerchiefs and messages for Agatha, asking her to make contact. Usually she would find a way to signal to them, but unbeknown to them, she had been confined to her cell.

"Why are *you* locked up in here? Aren't you allowed visitors?" asked Nancy, placing the handkerchief on the bed between them.

Agatha's face twisted into a dark frown. "I'm permitted no visitors – my husband saw to that. But now Charlotte has brought you back here and…" Her face collapsed in on itself like a deflating balloon. Agatha had only answered half of Nancy's question and she was about to ask again why she was locked up, when there was a quiet rap at the door. *The guard had returned.*

Nancy gave the door an anxious glance and stood up, her head still swimming with questions.

"I am so sorry about Charlotte, Nancy. I truly am." Agatha looked distraught as she gripped the edge of the bedframe.

"I must get Mother out of this place," said Nancy fiercely. "I know she's innocent. I think the mayor has falsely accused her."

"I think you are right," said Agatha, biting down on her bottom lip.

"Why would the mayor do that? Is he the reason you are in here too?" asked Nancy. She swiped at a tear on her cheek.

There was another *rap, rap, rap* on the door. "Come on, time's up," hissed the guard.

"This has gone on for too long," whispered Agatha, shaking her head. She stood up and grasped Nancy's hands. "Percival sent a letter to your grandfather, after things went so terribly wrong for our family. It was the reason you and your mother left to start a new life in Leeds. Ask your grandfather where the letter is. The time has come to show it to someone – perhaps it will help your mother. Tell him it *must* be done." Agatha's voice was urgent and low.

"Hurry," whispered the guard, tapping on the door again.

Nancy stared at Agatha, her head still bursting with questions, but she did not have time to ask them, for the guard opened the door, reached in and grabbed the back of her coat. With a single yank, he pulled her round the cell door, shutting and locking it behind her. "I said five minutes," he whispered, his voice tight with disappointment.

As Nancy followed the guard back down the stairs, her head was spinning with everything she had just learned. Her aunt was married to the horrible mayor, which must explain why his astronomy book had been in the cupola. She remembered the conversation she had overheard between the mayor and her grandfather in the apothecary shop. *"Your daughter got what she deserved."* It wasn't her mother the mayor had been talking about, but Agatha. The photograph of the couple standing in front of Cupola House she had seen in the mayor's house – it wasn't her mother arm-in-arm with the mayor, but her aunt. It was time to confront her grandfather with what she knew, and ask about the letter Agatha had mentioned. Nancy would not rest until she had learned the truth.

Chapter 28

Answers

"Gosh, Nancy. I thought the prison had swallowed you up and would never spit you out," said Burch, his face pinched with worry.

Nancy slumped against the wall, gulping in deep breaths of night air as the guard bolted the side door behind her.

"What happened in there?" asked Burch.

Nancy quietly told him about meeting her aunt, who had been in the prison for such a long time and was married to the mayor.

Burch gasped. "Are you sure she was telling you

the truth? I've lived in this town all my life and never heard anyone speak of the mayor's wife."

Nancy nodded. "I'm certain. Agatha looked so like Mother, there is no mistaking they are related. To think I have had an aunt all these years and knew nothing of her."

"Poor Mr Greenstone, two of his daughters locked up in prison," said Burch, whistling quietly through his teeth.

Nancy glanced at Burch. "Agatha didn't say why she was in prison, but it can't be a coincidence that my mother is now in there too. The mayor is behind this and I need to find out why and put a stop to it."

Burch's eyes became wide and owl-like in the dark. They walked in silence towards Cupola House, through the quiet streets where only occasional observers of the comet stood on their doorsteps quietly watching.

"If the mayor is behind it, then my pa did lie about seeing your ma start the fire," said Burch eventually, his voice small and thin.

Nancy looked at her friend. "I'm sorry to say it, Burch. I think he must have done."

Burch puffed out a long, slow breath, his eyes glued to the pavement as they walked. He stopped outside an inn, where the clink of glasses could be heard from an open window as the landlord cleared up. "At one time I'd have sworn on my life that Pa would not have done such a thing, but now I'm not so sure. It's bewildering how his character has changed."

"We must speak with him, see if he will tell us exactly what happened the night of the fire," said Nancy.

"Yes, we must," said Burch, his jaw clenched. "There's something else, Nancy. I can't stop thinking about the broken telescope in the town observatory. Why *hasn't* the mayor had it repaired for the comet party tomorrow?"

A sudden memory tugged at Nancy's brow. "When the mayor came into the haberdashery shop the day of Violet's accident, didn't he tell your father to go to the observatory to continue preparing for the party?"

"Yes, I think he might have done," said Burch. "Why do you ask?"

"The observatory can't be very big. Surely there are better suited rooms for the party preparations?" asked Nancy.

A muscle twitched in Burch's cheek. "You're right. Maybe that is a bit peculiar. Pa has a set of master keys to the Subscription Rooms. I'll try and borrow them without him noticing so I can have a look around. If you can meet me at eight o'clock tomorrow morning outside the Rooms, we can find Pa and see what he has to say. We'll try and look in the observatory too."

With that decided, the children hurried on through the night. "Agatha told me of something else that could help free my mother," said Nancy, going on to explain about the letter her aunt had spoken of.

"You must talk to Mr Greenstone as soon as you get back," urged Burch, as they neared Cupola House.

"I will," said Nancy, giving her friend a small smile. "I truly think we are a step closer to solving these mysteries, Burch. Tomorrow is going to be a better day for both of our families, I am certain of it."

Violet was snoring gently when Nancy returned to the house and their grandfather was in his room, presumably asleep. Nancy's limbs felt heavy with exhaustion, but her brain was as fizzy as a bottle of pop as she crept into the apothecary shop and stood in front of the herb drawers. *A teaspoon of chamomile and lemon balm, a pinch of ginger.* In the kitchen she ground the herbs and spice in a pestle and mortar, tied them up into a square of muslin cloth and made two mugs of fragrant tea. Quickly carrying the mugs upstairs, she placed them on the floor outside her grandfather's bedroom and knocked on his door. "Grandfather, you need to wake up."

The creak of bedsprings. "Nancy, it is very late, my dear. You should be in bed." His voice was croaky, as if it needed oiling.

"I need to talk to you," Nancy said urgently. "I know about my aunt, Agatha. I've seen her." She gulped in a deep breath, the scented steam of the tea soothing her nerves as she waited for her grandfather to reply.

Footsteps across the room. The door creaked open a crack. Grandfather stood there in his nightshirt, his fingers shaking as he fumbled with his spectacles. "What do you mean, you've seen her?" he whispered in disbelief. "Is she all right? I've been so worried."

"I think she's all right. I've been to the prison," Nancy said, suddenly feeling a little less brave.

"What!" Grandfather exclaimed; his cheeks creased in anguish. He stood back and ushered her inside.

Nancy picked up the mugs of tea and walked into his room, swallowing a gasp as she looked around. The warm glow of three oil lamps on the walls illuminated the heavy wooden furniture. Silver photograph frames of varying sizes dotted every surface: the bedside table, the mantel above the fireplace, the oak chest of drawers.

Nancy placed the mugs of tea on the bedside table, picked up a photograph and peered at it. A sepia image of two girls in long summer dresses and wide hats with gauzy ribbons. Their expressions were serious, but Nancy detected a glint in their eyes as if they were swallowing cheeky smiles. She placed it down and picked up another. Her grandfather beside the same two girls, older now, perhaps in their early twenties, standing outside Cupola House, next to a horse and cart with a board advertising *Greenstone's Apothecary Shop*.

"These photographs are of Mother and Agatha," whispered Nancy. Her grandfather had created a shrine to his two girls in his bedroom, a place where he could remember them in happier times.

Grandfather walked to his bed and sat on it with a heavy *whump*, the springs creaking in surprise. "How can you have seen Agatha at the prison? She is locked up," he whispered, shaking his head.

Nancy returned the photograph to the table, took the mug of tea her grandfather was offering her and sipped it, the warmth easing some of her tension. She stood before him, speaking slowly and steadily of her visit to the police station with Burch, how they had learned that Burch's father had witnessed her mother's supposed crime, and finally, her unexpected visit to the prison and the encounter with Agatha.

Nancy's grandfather placed his own mug of tea down with a bump, liquid sloshing over the side. "Prisons are dark and dangerous places; anything could have happened to you. All these years I have been trying to keep you safe and this happens!"

"But nothing happened. I am fine," said Nancy. "Can't you see? I had to try and contact Mother and do something to help."

Grandfather rubbed his sallow cheeks, his eyes suddenly sorrowful. "I fear that I've failed you and Violet. With your mother gone too I felt hopeless, retreated into my shell like a mollusc. I should have been there for you and your sister." He patted the crumpled sheets on his bed and Nancy placed the mug on the table and sat next to him. "I don't approve of what you've done, but you have been very determined in trying to resolve matters," he said, taking Nancy's hand and giving it a light squeeze. A wave of tiredness and emotion at the day's events spilled over her and she grasped his fingers, welcoming his warmth.

"Come here," he said gruffly.

She nestled into his side, her shoulders relaxing a little.

"You remind me of your mother and your aunt; you have their grit and determination," he said. "Tell me about Agatha. I've been so worried about her."

"There was unrest at the prison because of the comet. The prisoners are all locked in their cells," said Nancy, tilting her head to look up at him.

"Oh," said Grandfather with a frown, pushing his spectacles onto his nose. "That explains it. Your mother and I tried to get word to Agatha…"

"You sent more handkerchiefs and messages to see if she was all right?" interrupted Nancy.

"Yes," said Grandfather, looking a little bewildered at what Nancy had discovered. "But none of the usual people would help or even speak to us. I suppose that was because of the unrest." He paused. "What else did Agatha say to you?"

"She told me she is married to the mayor. I saw a photograph through a window in the mayor's house. It looked a little like Mother and the mayor standing in front of Cupola House, but now I know it was Agatha," said Nancy. "Is the mayor the reason she is in prison? What happened?"

The crevices in Grandfather's forehead deepened. "I had something the mayor wanted very badly, and I would not give it to him."

He reached across and picked up the photograph of Nancy's mother and Agatha standing outside Cupola House. He held the silver frame tightly, his eyes damp and overly bright. Nancy leaned in closer, waiting for him to reveal the truth she had been so desperate to discover.

Chapter 29

The Letter

Nancy perched on the bed beside her grandfather as he began to speak, his voice low as he clutched the photograph of his two daughters. "The mayor wanted Cupola House and I would not give it to him. That was the start of all of our troubles," he said. Nancy leaned away in surprise, waiting for her grandfather to continue. "When Percival began courting Agatha, he was not mayor but he was ambitious and I felt he would stop at nothing to get what he wanted. But despite his ambition, he was charming and treated Agatha with affection and she quickly fell in love with him."

Nancy remembered seeing the mayor cheerfully greet the two women walking to church. If he had revealed this charming side of his character to her aunt, Nancy could see how this might have happened. "Did the mayor love Agatha too?"

"I think Percival loved the fact that she would inherit this house," replied Grandfather sadly, placing the photograph back on the table. "After their engagement, I allowed Percival to escort Agatha upstairs to the cupola where they would watch the night and stargaze. Your mother would accompany them. But, on one of these occasions, she overheard Percival say that one day this house would be his and Agatha's. He said that the cupola was the highest point in town and quite magnificent, that it would be a fitting place for him to watch and rule over his people when he was mayor. Your mother told me this, and I felt Percival's self-importance was getting out of hand." Grandfather paused and grasped his knees, his hands trembling. "And after he and Agatha married, I was proved right."

"Why? What happened?" asked Nancy, hardly daring to blink in case she missed something.

"Percival and Agatha moved to a small cottage on the edge of town, but whenever they visited me, Percival would speak of the changes he wished to make to Cupola House. He wanted to close the apothecary shop and run the town from here when he became mayor."

"But how could he do that when you own the house?" asked Nancy, pushing away a horrible image of her grandfather's plants, potions and possessions being marched from the house.

"Agatha is my eldest daughter, and everything will eventually pass to her and her husband. When Percival was elected mayor many years ago, his head became as swollen as a hornets' nest. He demanded that he and Agatha have the house and that I, and you and your mother, move to their cottage. Agatha protested strongly but he would not listen."

"But that wasn't fair," said Nancy hotly.

"It was a terrible time," said her grandfather, shaking his head. "Agatha was torn in two and grew very unhappy. I spoke to both of my daughters and we decided my will should be changed. We thought if Percival knew there was no opportunity of inheriting the house, he might accept matters and he and Agatha could move on with their married lives."

"What happened after that?" asked Nancy.

"Percival was as venomous as a snake when he

learned what I had done. As a consequence, Agatha became even more miserable. But her one small joy was helping your mother care for you."

"I wish I remembered this," said Nancy in a small voice. "I have no memories of Agatha or the mayor at all."

"And that is for the best," said Nancy's grandfather, giving her a slightly strange look, as if something was hidden behind his words.

"What has this got to do with Agatha being in prison?" asked Nancy.

Grandfather frowned. "There was a fire at Agatha and Percival's cottage." He paused and looked at Nancy. "Percival accused Agatha of starting the fire and had her arrested."

Nancy pressed her palms into her thighs. *Another fire.* "Was the fire Agatha's fault?"

Grandfather shook his head. He looked at his hands. "No, it was an accident."

"But that's dreadful," said Nancy. "Couldn't anything be done to prove it was an accident?"

"No," said her grandfather, picking at the loose skin near a thumbnail. "We tried everything."

Nancy thought about the photograph she had seen

of Agatha and the mayor. "But if the mayor feels so badly towards Agatha, why would he still have a picture of her in his house?"

"I expect he doesn't even notice my dear daughter in that photograph," said Grandfather sadly. "It is the house in the photograph he cares for, not her."

What dreadfully sad events, thought Nancy. The mayor had devoted half of his life to destroying her grandfather and those he loved because he could not get what he wanted, and her aunt had been in prison for years because of it. But Agatha had mentioned a way things might be put right. "Agatha spoke of a letter the mayor sent to you, said that was the reason Mother and I left all those years ago. She said we should show it to someone, that it might help free Mother," said Nancy. "Surely this letter could help Agatha too?"

Her grandfather's eyes darkened.

"What does the letter say?" asked Nancy. "Please, Grandfather. Agatha said it was important."

Grandfather sighed and stood up. "You have learned the truth of the situation, so I suppose seeing the letter the mayor wrote to me after he put Agatha in prison will not hurt." He walked over to a chest of drawers, opened the bottom drawer and lifted a pile of woolly jumpers.

Pulling something out from underneath them, he walked over and handed a piece of paper to Nancy, and she began to read.

I have lost my cottage and everything that I have worked for because of you and your daughter. Your decision to cut me from your will was ill-judged and I am determined you shall suffer in the way I suffer now. Do not underestimate the power I have over the people of this town, or how difficult I can make life for you and your family. You will all pay for what has happened, you can be sure of that, and if you show this letter to another living soul, you will only make matters worse for those you hold dear.

"Gosh," said Nancy, her eyes widening. The mayor had threatened not only her grandfather, but his family as well, and was intent on seeking revenge. "But why didn't you show this letter to someone before? The police may have been able to help," she said, passing it back to her grandfather.

He took the paper from her and folded it quickly. "The letter is neither addressed to me, nor signed. It would not have proved a thing. Besides, Agatha begged us to keep it secret. She knew the true force of the mayor's personality and had no doubt his threats were real."

"But Agatha's changed her mind, Grandfather. She truly believes showing this letter to someone will help!" said Nancy in frustration.

"Think of the mayor's final sentence, Nancy. What would he do to me, or you and Violet, if he knew you were staying here, if he found out I'd showed the letter to someone?" said Grandfather, shaking his head. "The mayor came to visit me in the shop again early yesterday morning and I had an inkling he had somehow discovered your mother was back. I was right. He sent an invitation, asking your mother and me to visit his house last night – around the time the burning handkerchief was pushed through his letter box. We decided to accept his invitation in the hope we could persuade him to free Agatha and leave our family be."

"And he refused?" said Nancy.

"Not outright," said Grandfather. "We were hopeful he might have thought about it after our meeting, but when the police came knocking at our door the next morning, I realized he'd no intention of leaving us be.

He was still intent on destroying our family. In fact, he had set us up."

"You and Mother should have protested her innocence more strongly to the police," said Nancy hotly.

Grandfather shook his head. "It would have made matters worse. And there was you and Violet to think of."

Nancy's chin wobbled as she remembered her mother placing a silencing finger to her lips, just before walking into the shop to face the police. She had wanted minimal fuss to keep her children safe. "We have to do *something*, Grandfather," Nancy said, thinking fast. "Burch's father has been treated terribly by the mayor too. He could have been forced by the mayor to lie about seeing Mother start the fire."

"It's possible," said Grandfather, standing up and returning the letter to its hiding place in his bottom drawer.

"If Burch's father saw this letter, it might make him feel less alone, persuade him to speak up and tell the truth," said Nancy, following him.

Grandfather closed the drawer and turned to look at her. "No, Nancy. My two daughters are in prison and if the mayor finds out I have shown this letter to anyone, I fear one of us could be next."

Nancy stared at her grandfather in dismay. He was still afraid of the mayor and firmly within the man's clutches. The secrets and lies surrounding the mayor were scattered like branches on a woodland floor after a storm. But the pathway was beginning to look a little clearer and the more she thought of it, the more certain Nancy was of what she needed to do. The letter was solid evidence of the mayor's poor treatment of her family. If Burch's father saw it, he might just be persuaded to tell the truth about the fire and then they might be able to unravel everything else the mayor had done too.

"You must tell no one you have seen the letter, Nancy," Grandfather said again. "Agatha was sadly mistaken when she said it would help resolve matters. If that was the case, I would have used it before now."

Nancy tucked her elbows into her sides and did not reply. She would not lie, but she would not tell her grandfather the truth either. If her plan did not work, he would be none the wiser. But if it did work, her actions might just save them all.

CHAPTER 30

The Observatory

The next morning Nancy rose early, anxious to be on time for her eight o'clock meeting with Burch outside the Subscription Rooms. Grandfather woke up early too and prepared Nancy and Violet a breakfast of kippers and poached eggs from the leftover provisions. "I shall quickly clean the shop, then take a walk. There is something I must do," he said, his eyes a little brighter than the previous evening.

"Something to help Mother?" asked Violet, through a mouthful of kipper.

"Yes," Grandfather replied. "It's something I should

have done yesterday morning, when the police came knocking on our door. Stay inside and try to keep yourselves busy. I will see you later." He gave them both affectionate pats on the shoulders, then disappeared into the shop. The sound of the brush sweeping across the floor and the clink of bottles and jars made Nancy feel relieved he was no longer in his room lost in his memories and thoughts.

Nancy had wondered whether it would frighten Violet to learn of the previous day's events, but then she remembered how unsettled they had both felt when their mother had been hiding things from them. She decided the time for secrets was over and Violet must know the whole truth.

"But the mayor has treated our aunt terribly," said Violet after Nancy had finished recounting the events. "We must tell the police."

"It's not as simple as that," said Nancy. "The mayor is cunning as a fox and we need firm evidence to prove his bad deeds." She patted her apron pocket, feeling the hard edges of the mayor's letter she had retrieved from her grandfather's bedroom early that morning. While Violet was getting dressed and Grandfather was preparing breakfast, she had snuck into his room, her fingers trembling with the worry of being caught. She sorely hoped the letter would provide the evidence needed to begin to resolve matters. "I need to go out on a quick errand, Violet," said Nancy, glancing at the clock. It was seven-thirty and she did not want to be late for Burch. Today was supposed to be their last day in this town. If the situation couldn't be resolved, Father would soon need to be told. Her head throbbed at the realization of how badly things had gone.

"Can I come?" asked Violet.

"I'm not sure that's a good idea." Nancy did not know how Mr Cavendish might react and she did not want to put her sister in any danger.

"Is this to do with the mayor?" asked Violet, frowning.

"Yes. You'll be safer here in the house."

Violet shook her head vehemently. "I hate the mayor as much as you do. And if *you* might not be safe then I'm coming. Sisters should stick together."

Nancy thought of her mother and Agatha, two sisters torn apart. The thought of being parted from Violet for years and years like that made all of her limbs feel restless and jumpy. She did not want to lie to her sister about the plan to confront Burch's father. In fact, the thought of sharing the burden loosened some of the tension in her jaw. "All right, you can come. Sisters *should* stick together no matter what. Now listen carefully, and I'll tell you what Burch and I intend to do."

Abbeygate Street was as clean as a new penny, flags fluttering like clapping hands, highly polished windows beaming in delight. Every building was buffed, dressed and ready for the comet party. An air of excitement and expectation at the festivities buzzed from every home, shop and business. Tonight the comet would be at its closest point to Earth – a mere fourteen million miles away. Nancy glanced at Mr Thompson's putty-edged door and thought of the couple they had met on the train with their gas masks. It seemed few people here feared the comet gas, and that most had a sense of giddy anticipation.

The bell in a nearby church tolled eight o'clock as Nancy and Violet hurried towards the Subscription Rooms. On a small balcony above the entrance to the two-storey, cream-painted building, a brass telescope was being assembled and polished. Above this, a small, green, hat-like dome sat low on the roof. It had to be the town observatory.

251

"Where is Burch?" Nancy said under her breath, as they stood and watched people hurrying about, carrying trays of vegetables and fruit, vases of pearly white hot-house blooms and crates of champagne into the building. With a lurch Nancy noticed the mayor's red car parked outside, paintwork gleaming, its tyres as white as moons. Her nerves jangled at the thought of the mayor striding towards her, demanding to know who she was and why she had been peering through the windows of his house the day before. What would he do if he discovered the truth? She was putting both herself and Violet in danger, but she could not turn back; it was vital they got to the bottom of Mr Cavendish's lie and helped their mother and their aunt.

"Maybe Burch has already gone inside?" said Violet.

"Perhaps," said Nancy, slipping her hand into Violet's and following a woman carrying an armful of pressed tablecloths into the building. The woman took a left turn and disappeared through a set of double doors.

Violet was looking around in wide-eyed delight. "Look, Nancy," she said, pointing above the doors straight ahead of them. Silver-painted rubber balloons had been fashioned into the shape of a comet above the doorway. Balloons were a rarity and to see so many at once was an extraordinary sight. But this was no time to be distracted.

Nancy tugged on her sister's hand and they followed the woman with the tablecloths, soon finding themselves in the ballroom. Nancy paused for a second. She heard Violet puff out a small breath. A dazzling chandelier hung from the curved, pale-green ceiling, smaller chandeliers radiating out from it. They blinked like diamonds as the morning sun streamed in from the high windows to their left. A wooden viewing platform had been constructed along the length of the windows and upon it stood half-a-dozen large brass telescopes. Round dining tables were being set up with stiff linen cloths and polished silver cutlery. It seemed that no expense had been spared for this party – those with tickets were to be treated to a truly wondrous occasion.

Nancy glanced at the people preparing the party; they were scurrying around the ballroom like ants. Her eyes settled on each person in turn as she searched for Burch and his father.

A tap on her right shoulder.

Nancy started; turned round. But it wasn't the mayor,

just the harassed-looking woman who had been carrying the tablecloths.

"Can I help you, Miss?" she said.

"Oh, we are looking for Burch Cavendish," said Nancy quickly.

"What do you want with him?" she asked with a frown.

"Um…we have a message for him," said Nancy.

The woman's frown deepened as she glanced at Violet. "Burch is helping Mr Thompson carry crates of champagne upstairs to the bar. But you children really shouldn't be in here…" There was a sudden crash and Nancy turned to see a glass vase on the floor and a red-cheeked girl standing in a puddle of water. With a shake of her head, the woman turned abruptly and strode off towards the commotion. "What's happened?" she barked. "You know how careful the mayor told us to be with costs…we cannot afford to replace broken items."

"Quick," hissed Nancy, steering Violet to the sweeping staircase to their right, which led to a balcony overlooking the ballroom. The sharpness of the woman's voice followed them as they ran up the stairs. Reaching the top, Nancy scanned the ballroom for the mayor, but he was nowhere to be seen. "Come on, this way," she said, leading her sister from the balcony into a long corridor.

The clink of bottles was coming from an open door halfway down. Walking swiftly to the door, she and Violet peeped inside. A man was pulling bottles of champagne from straw-filled crates. A pyramid of sparkling champagne glasses stacked on a white-clothed table by the window made Nancy blink in amazement.

"Excuse me…we're looking for Burch Cavendish," said Nancy, tearing her eyes away from the glasses and looking at the man. "We were told he might be in here."

The man looked up. "He took a tray of champagne glasses to the reading room, two doors down on the right."

"Thank you," said Nancy, giving the man a nod. This was taking longer than she had expected; they needed to hurry before the woman downstairs came looking for them and Grandfather noticed they were gone.

"Look," said Violet, as they approached the closed door to the reading room. A tray of champagne glasses stood on the floor. Nancy hovered outside and heard voices behind the door. She pressed a finger to her lips to signal Violet to be quiet.

"I shall present the cheque to the charity foundation at ten o'clock this evening," said a voice Nancy instantly recognized.

"It's the mayor," Nancy whispered and she felt Violet tense at her side.

"I want all partygoers gathered in the ballroom to see me do this from the balcony. Make sure there are no distractions," the mayor continued.

"Yes, Mayor," said another voice that Nancy recognized. *Mr Cavendish.* His tone was dull and heavy as a stone.

"Come now, Cavendish. Why so glum? This is a very good day indeed." The mayor's voice sounded full of self-satisfaction.

Violet tugged on Nancy's hand. "Come away, Nancy. What if he comes out and sees us listening?" Her voice was small and a little afraid.

Nancy felt a sudden rush of guilt at bringing Violet here and allowed her sister to lead her down the corridor and away from the reading room. A man carrying a crate gave them a quick glance as he walked past, then continued on to the bar. Nancy glanced back at the tray of champagne glasses on the floor. Burch had been here but had now vanished. Then she remembered his idea to look in the observatory. She thought about the green copper dome on the roof. They must be standing in the middle of the building, almost directly beneath it. She had not yet seen an entrance to the observatory, so it must be ahead of them. "Come on," whispered Nancy, half running along the corridor.

"Where are we going?" asked Violet.

"We're looking for an entrance to the rooftop observatory," said Nancy. "I think that's where we'll find Burch."

"I'll look to the right, you look to the left," said Violet determinedly.

Though she was wary about leaving her little sister alone, Nancy knew they were running out of time. At the end of the corridor Nancy took a left turn, her eyes skimming over the doors. None of them seemed likely to lead to the observatory.

Two women carrying crystal vases of pink globe-like flowers chattered as they walked past, but they ignored Nancy and Violet.

"Over here!" called Violet quietly, when the women had gone.

Nancy saw her sister standing by a door set back into an alcove that was smaller than the others and ran over.

A sign on the door said: *Observatory – Strictly No Admittance*. This was it! Nancy tried the door handle. It was locked. She stared at it in disappointment. She heard a burst of laughter and glanced back along the corridor. The mayor and Mr Cavendish could emerge from the reading room at any second. "Can you keep watch? Tell me if you see anyone coming?" Nancy asked Violet.

Violet nodded, ran quickly along the wall and peeped round the corner. "It's all clear," she whispered.

Nancy rapped on the door to the observatory and waited. She was met with silence. *Come on, Burch. Where are you?* She rapped again. There was the sound of footsteps bumping on stairs. Then more silence, but she sensed someone was behind the door, listening. "Burch? Is that you?" she said in a low voice. There was the sound of keys clinking, then the lock turned and Nancy stood back, her hands trembling a little, as the door opened.

Burch's face peered round the door. He was holding a ring of keys.

"What are you doing in there?" asked Violet, peering round Burch to the steep stairs behind him.

"Why didn't you meet us outside?" asked Nancy.

"People were hovering by the door. I couldn't get out," Burch explained. He was breathing heavily, his eyes glassy and Nancy did not think it was because he had just run down the stairs.

"Have you found something?" whispered Nancy.

Burch nodded. "You need to come and see," he said, gesturing for them to follow him. "But it's not good, Nancy. It's not good at all."

Chapter 31

Confrontation

Nancy followed Violet and Burch up the narrow stairs and through a half-moon-shaped trapdoor into the small observatory. She sucked in the warm, musty air and looked around in amazement. The walls, ceiling and floor were constructed of wooden planks, and it felt a little like being inside a giant barrel. A round porthole let in a circle of light that illuminated the celestial charts pinned to the walls and the large white telescope which was bolted to the floor.

Burch kneeled beside the telescope, chewing on his bottom lip. He watched as Nancy's eyes were drawn to the gap in the floor by his knees.

Violet gasped. "What's in there?" she asked, staring at the objects hidden under the floorboards – four metal boxes nestling next to each other.

"Money," said Burch, opening the lid of a box to reveal stacks of banknotes. "Lots and lots of it. When I got up here one of the floorboards was sticking up, and some pliers were resting next to it. I pulled up the board and found the cash boxes."

"But why hasn't the money been put in the bank?" asked Violet, as she and Nancy crouched beside Burch.

"There's only one reason it would be hidden like this. It must be stolen," said Nancy.

"Look at that," said Violet, pointing to a handwritten note stuck to the inside of a cash box. *Fifty per cent of Comet Party ticket sales, May 1910.*

Nancy opened the other two cash boxes and saw identical notes had been stuck to the inside lids.

"That's my pa's handwriting," said Burch, his words catching in his throat.

Nancy felt as if a light had been switched on in her head. "Your father must have been stealing the money he's collected for the party," she said, feeling a little sick.

Burch sat back on his heels and ground his palms into his eyes. "But Pa's been taking the ticket money to the bank; I even saw him in there one day."

"He wasn't banking all of it," said Nancy, looking at her friend. Burch had said his father was an honest man. But, then again, he had lied about seeing her mother start the fire so perhaps he was mistaken.

There was the sudden rapid thump of feet on the stairs below the observatory. "Who's up there?" called an anxious voice.

"My pa. I forgot to lock the observatory door," whispered Burch, his jaw twitching. He picked up a cash box and stood up. "I have to ask him about this."

Nancy took short, shallow breaths as they waited for Mr Cavendish's head to emerge through the trapdoor. What would he say when he found out they knew his secret? They were trapped up here with no way out. She pulled Violet a little closer, suddenly fearful.

When Mr Cavendish finally appeared, sweat was peppering his brow. "Burch!" he exclaimed. "And you two," he said, looking at Nancy and Violet in surprise. "So it was you who took my keys, Burch! I've been so anxious about what the mayor would say when he knew they were missing…" His voice trailed off as he noticed the pulled-up floorboards and the cash box in Burch's hands. He sucked on his teeth. "You must leave immediately, forget what you have seen here and tell no one," he said urgently.

Burch held the cash box close to his chest. "What is this, Pa? You need to tell me the truth. Have you been stealing? Is that why you've not been yourself these past months?"

Mr Cavendish strode over to Burch, took the cash box, then kneeled and laid it next to the others. He picked up the floorboards and began to slide them back into place. "You need to leave," he whispered again, glancing at the trapdoor anxiously. "Quick, before he comes."

"Tell us, Pa. Tell us the truth," demanded Burch.

Mr Cavendish returned the final floorboard, wiped his sweaty brow on his jacket sleeve, and stood up. "I can't. You must go, all of you."

"No. We're not leaving until you tell us what has been going on," said Nancy, her fear making her bold. "I know you lied about seeing my mother start the fire at the mayor's house."

Mr Cavendish stared at Nancy. "She's your *mother*? You're Mr Greenstone's granddaughters?" Nancy nodded.

Mr Cavendish let out a small moan. "I'm so sorry. I didn't want to lie; you must believe me."

"So why did you?" asked Nancy, feeling a jolt of relief that at least he had confessed to something.

Mr Cavendish gave Nancy a small and sorrowful look and rubbed his cheeks. "It's a tangled mess I've found myself in, and I fear there's no way out."

Burch faced his father, his bottom lip trembling. "Nancy and Violet's ma is falsely imprisoned because of you. Help us, please. You have to tell us what you know."

Mr Cavendish bowed his head and puffed out a long sigh. "You were so keen to come up here and look through the telescope, Burch, you spoke of nothing else for weeks."

"What's that got to do with anything?" asked Burch in surprise.

Mr Cavendish placed a trembling hand on the barrel of the telescope. "I wanted to arrange a visit to the observatory for your school. It was to be a surprise. When I saw the mayor's motor car outside the Subscription Rooms early one morning, I came in to enquire if it might be possible. I found the mayor in the observatory with the cash boxes and quickly worked out what was going on. He threatened to ruin me if I told anyone what I'd seen, said he'd tell folks that *I'd* been stealing the money and storing it up here. He takes a cut of the money from every party he holds, uses it to buy fine things; his motor car, fancy clothes, furnishings for his house. His greed makes him take full advantage of his position of power."

"Oh, Pa!" exclaimed Burch. "And no one ever suspects a thing because he's the mayor."

"And he's bold enough to label the cash boxes because he never thought he'd be caught," said Nancy quietly.

Mr Cavendish hung his head and gave a limp nod. "He lied about the telescope being broken, so he could store the money up here."

"But why store it up here at all?" asked Burch with a frown.

"I've wondered the same thing," said Mr Cavendish.

"Gosh," said Violet quietly.

Thoughts were gathering in Nancy's head, one after the other like a needle running through fabric. "When you discovered the mayor stealing the money, he forced you to work for him and to lie about seeing our mother set his house alight," she said, realizing that the mayor's actions had entangled the fortunes of the Greenstone and Cavendish families in a terrible way.

"So you being a false witness was the urgent task the mayor wanted to speak to you about?" asked Burch.

"You read the mayor's note," stated Mr Cavendish dully.

"I'm sorry, Pa. I was worried about you," said Burch.

Mr Cavendish let out a long sigh and nodded. "The mayor planned to set fire to a handkerchief and push it through his own letter box, just after a prearranged visit from Mr Greenstone and his daughter. He told me I must go to the police and say I'd seen Charlotte Greenstone do it, and that the handkerchief belonged to her."

"No," gasped Nancy.

"What!" exclaimed Violet.

"You should have stood up to the mayor and refused, Pa," said Burch tightly. "That's what you would have told me to do."

Mr Cavendish gave his son an anguished look. "The mayor has a way with words that makes you feel small. His threats are very real. You only need to see how Mr Greenstone's been rejected by the folks of this town to understand the mayor's power. You must swear you'll tell no one about what you've discovered up here. It would ruin our family, and yours too," he whispered, nodding at Nancy.

Nancy looked at Mr Cavendish in dismay. "But my family's lives have already been ruined," she said. If he didn't speak up, then their mother would remain in prison, and justice needed to be served.

"I'm sorry, but you must swear not to tell a living soul about this," Mr Cavendish urged them again.

Violet looked at Nancy.

Burch rubbed the back of his neck.

Nancy thought of her father. If he were here now, she was certain he would try and persuade Mr Cavendish to speak up. The mayor's lies and threats needed to be brought to a stop. She pulled the mayor's letter to her grandfather from her apron pocket with shaking fingers, Violet and Burch watching her with wide eyes. "The mayor has a hold on you, just as he does my family. He sent this letter to my grandfather threatening us. Please put a stop to this and help free our mother."

"Please help our mother come home," added Violet in a small voice. "We miss her ever so much." She pushed her hands into the pockets of her dress and looked at Mr Cavendish hopefully.

Mr Cavendish's eyes were watery as he took the letter from Nancy and skimmed the words. He wiped his nose on the back of his hand. "I'm sorry your family's been treated badly by the mayor too. But how can I confess the truth about your mother when the mayor has sworn to ruin *my* family?"

"And ruin you I will if you speak any more of this." The mayor's voice curled through the trapdoor opening and into the observatory like smoke.

Nancy gasped and clapped a hand to her mouth.

Violet clutched for Nancy's other hand.

Burch stumbled into the telescope with a bump.

Mr Cavendish's eyes grew very wide as the mayor climbed into the observatory. The mayor's steely gaze settled on Nancy, Violet and Burch and then flickered to Mr Cavendish and the letter in his hand. A thunderbolt of fear arched up Nancy's spine as she waited for the mayor's next move. She did not have to wait for long. The mayor swept the letter from Mr Cavendish's fingers with ease, his eyes narrowing as he read it. He peered at Nancy. "You have been busy, Nancy. Visiting Agatha. Looking through the windows of my home. Prising the truth from Cavendish."

A rush of dizziness made Nancy wobble. *The mayor knew who she was and what she had been doing!*

"Don't look so surprised," the mayor said, his voice as slippery as satin. "You bear a striking resemblance to your mother and your aunt, and seeing your handkerchief in the haberdashery merely confirmed things. It is such a pity your mother decided to return and that you decided to meddle in my affairs. Quite a number of those handkerchiefs have been delivered to Agatha in prison over the years, and I have had quite a number intercepted too. I must say, the needlework is quite…fine."

A rising horror blurred Nancy's vision as she remembered the red-edged handkerchief she had used on Violet's elbow after her near miss with the motor car the day after their arrival. The mayor had picked up the handkerchief in the haberdashery and passed it to her. They should have heeded Mother's wishes to stay inside, for her and Violet's first outing had unknowingly exposed who they were. Blood rushed to her cheeks at the thought of the mayor intercepting the stitched handkerchiefs intended for Agatha, then setting light to one in order to implicate her mother.

The mayor gave Nancy and Violet a sickly-sweet smile. "It is most disappointing that Mr Greenstone went against my wishes and shared this private letter with you. Agatha's prison sentence is soon to be reviewed, but I am sure the prison board can be persuaded to extend it for a few more years."

"No!" exclaimed Nancy.

Violet stood by her side, pinch-faced.

Burch glared at the mayor. "You can't do that," he said through gritted teeth. "I shall tell the police."

The mayor's laugh was reed-thin. "You really think they would believe you, Burch? You are a delivery boy! A quick word from me to tell the police you are pilfering while doing your deliveries and you too will be in trouble with the law."

Burch looked desperately to his father for help, but Mr Cavendish's eyes were fixed on his shoes.

"You're a bully," Nancy said, lifting her chin. "You made Mr Cavendish lie about seeing our mother start the fire at your house and you must release her from prison immediately."

"That is a very serious accusation, Nancy. Do you have any evidence to prove it?" said the mayor with a smirk.

Nancy willed Mr Cavendish to stand up to the mayor, but his head remained bowed.

"Cavendish. Did you see Charlotte Greenstone start the fire at my house?" said the mayor calmly.

Mr Cavendish continued to look down.

With every ounce of strength in her body, Nancy now willed him to speak up.

"Well, Cavendish?" said the mayor.

"Yes," whispered Mr Cavendish.

"Louder," demanded the mayor, his eyes cold and flinty.

"Yes," said Mr Cavendish more loudly, his words bouncing off the curved wooden ceiling.

All of Nancy's hope sank through the floor.

"Now, what to do with this?" the mayor said coolly as he looked at the letter in his hand. He reached into his pocket and pulled out a matchbox.

A slow-dawning horror clenched Nancy's jaw as she watched the mayor take out a match and strike it, the flame flickering as he held it to the corner of the brittle paper.

"No," she said, lurching forward, but the mayor whipped the letter away from her grasp, the flame devouring the paper and turning it to ash. He dropped the final burning corner to the floor and stamped out the flame with the heel of a well-polished shoe.

"Now, children. Kindly leave my observatory so that Cavendish can carry on with his duties," said the mayor, looking at them as if they were no more than irritating flies to be swatted away.

"Let's go," said Burch in a low voice, not looking at his father.

Nancy saw the mayor's eyes flicker to the floorboards covering the hidden cash boxes, then settle on poor Mr Cavendish whose stooped shoulders were trembling. She blinked back hot tears as she and Violet headed for the trapdoor opening. What would Grandfather say when he learned that the letter, taken against his wishes, had been destroyed? The mayor had threatened in the letter to make life worse for her family if it was shown to anyone. She had a feeling all of their lives were about to take an even worse turn, and the awful truth was that she only had herself to blame.

272

CHAPTER 32

Truth

As Nancy, Violet and Burch walked back up Abbeygate Street, excited conversations about the coming evening's comet party seemed to be spilling from the lips of every passer-by. To Nancy, it seemed as if the comet had whisked her along on a journey of her own which had now come to an abrupt end. Their plan to persuade Mr Cavendish to tell the truth had failed. The letter the mayor had sent to her grandfather had been destroyed. The only thing to be done was to contact her father and ask him to come and help. She imagined his cheeks contorting as he learned that

Mother was accused of a terrible crime and locked up in a cold, dark cell. But she needed him to take control, for Nancy felt out of her depth, like she was trying to stay afloat on a swollen river.

"I'm sorry for what my pa did, and that he won't confess," said Burch after a while, his voice pulsating with anger.

"This is all the mayor's doing," said Nancy bitterly. "He bullied your father into lying." She saw the comet banner strung high above the entrance to Abbeygate Street. "I can't believe that as well as the bullying he has been pocketing the ticket sales for his own ends. He is perfectly horrid."

"The money belongs to charity," said Violet crossly. "We need to stop him from taking it."

Burch came to a stop outside the haberdashery, almost bumping into two women comparing notes about the fine dresses they would be wearing to the party. "The mayor doesn't know that *we* know about the stolen money."

"Who would believe us if we told them?" said Nancy with a frown. "Violet and I have our mother and our aunt in prison and the mayor has threatened to keep Agatha locked up for longer. My grandfather has been shunned by the town because of him. And he still has a grip on your father and even threatened *your* reputation if you talk to the police."

Burch looked at Nancy. "We just give up then. I'm dreading going to the mayor's party tonight knowing what I do."

Nancy gave a limp shrug and turned away, staring glumly into the shop window. Mrs Cavendish had strung blue bunting around the edges of the glass, a blazing silver comet embroidered onto each triangle of cloth. Nancy's head throbbed. Her father said that justice was always brought upon those who did wrong, but he was mistaken. She thought again of the small pile of ash on the floor of the observatory; the destroyed letter. The mayor was too strong and powerful to be beaten. There was nothing to be done.

Nancy and Violet returned to Cupola House to find their grandfather pacing around his potted herbs on the first-floor landing. "I returned from my walk to find you gone, girls! Wherever have you been?" he said anxiously.

Violet sat on the stairs, her fingers fidgeting in her lap as Nancy stood before Grandfather, telling him of the morning's events. His cheeks turned from peachy pink to puce in a matter of seconds.

"I am sorry," said Nancy, tears building behind her eyes. "I know I was wrong to disobey you, leave the house and take the letter from your bedroom. I thought it might help Mr Cavendish confess to lying about seeing Mother start the fire. But he wouldn't and now the letter's gone and..." She paused and looked up at her grandfather's glittering eyes. He slowly stepped forward and took Nancy's hands in his. His palms were cool and gentle. She blinked, feeling the trickle of a tear on her cheek.

"The mayor knows who you are and burned the letter?" Grandfather asked softly.

Nancy nodded, lowering her head.

"The mayor is stealing the ticket money from the comet party and Mr Cavendish discovered this?"

Nancy nodded again.

"The mayor forced Mr Cavendish to lie about seeing your mother start the fire, but Mr Cavendish does not have the courage to own up?"

"Yes!" exclaimed Violet.

"Mr Cavendish will not admit the truth and the mayor will make life worse for us all because of what

I have done," whispered Nancy. Hopelessness bowed her shoulders and at that moment the only thing she wished for was her father to stride up the stairs, fold her into his arms and tell her everything would be all right. But things were so far from being all right, she could not see how even her father could make things better.

"The truth is important to you, my dear, isn't it?" asked her grandfather, with a frown.

"But of course," said Nancy, her voice thick with tears. "Father says we must not be afraid to raise our voices to fight for injustice. I did try...but I failed."

"Your father sounds like a wise and sensible man," said Nancy's grandfather. He gave Nancy's hands a squeeze. "When I was a boy my mother used to tell me to do what is right, not what is easy. I fear that...I fear that I may not have heeded her advice too well."

Nancy looked up at her grandfather, who was blinking rather rapidly behind his spectacles.

"My dears, there is something else I must tell you," he said, leading Nancy to the stairs and sitting her next to Violet. He gestured for them both to move along so he could sit down too, placed an arm around Nancy's shoulders and pulled her close, his breathing suddenly heavy. "Your actions over the past few days came from a good place in your heart, because you wanted to try and mend things. I appreciate your honesty and good intentions, even if things did not work out as you'd hoped." Grandfather paused and gave Nancy a gentle look. "But your mother and I have not been entirely honest with you, and you have made me see that we should have been. There is something we have kept from you – the whole truth of why you and your mother left this house all those years ago."

"You said we left because of threats the mayor made to our family," Nancy said, looking up at her grandfather. He had a far-away look again, as if he had stepped back into his memories.

Grandfather nodded. "That part is true. But there is something that the mayor doesn't know. Something that happened the night his cottage burned to the ground and Agatha was arrested."

Nancy felt a fluttering sensation in her chest, like a trapped butterfly. She reached for Violet's hand and waited for her grandfather to speak.

278

CHAPTER 33

Candle

Grandfather closed his eyes and began to speak slowly, Nancy and Violet listening intently as they sat beside him on the stairs holding hands. "February 1901 was long and cold. I'd recently changed my will so that Agatha and Percival would no longer inherit Cupola House. They were living in the cottage on the outskirts of town and Agatha had been to visit me in recent weeks, utterly miserable. She said Percival had been in a rage since he'd learned he would not inherit the house and was making her life a waking misery. He belittled her at every opportunity and gave her such meagre money for housekeeping that Agatha barely had enough to put meals on the table. And when she did, he said her food was inedible and would storm out of the house. You were almost two, Nancy, and your mother would often take you to visit Agatha to try and console her when Percival was out. Agatha took great delight in looking after you, would knit blankets and mittens and play with you endlessly."

"Did she embroider the pillowslip I found in the cot upstairs?" asked Nancy in a small voice.

"She did," said Grandfather with a distant smile. "The day of the cottage fire, your mother needed to run some errands. She asked if I would take you to spend a few hours with Agatha. But when we arrived, I saw that something wasn't right – the front door of the cottage was wide open. I picked you up and carried you into the hallway, which was so cold our breath steamed in front of us. I heard someone sobbing in the drawing room and I pushed the door open to see Agatha kneeling on the floor. Papers were strewn all around the room, as if a wind had come in and whipped them into a frenzy."

"Oh," said Violet. "Poor Agatha. What had happened?"

Grandfather cleared his throat. "Well, I put Nancy down by the fireplace and went to tend to Agatha. Through her tears she told me she'd had the most fearsome disagreement with Percival over his mean and cold-hearted ways and that she felt she could no longer live with him. I told her to pack a bag and return to live with us at Cupola House."

"Good," said Nancy.

Grandfather grimaced. "I'm afraid that isn't where the story ends. There was a sudden noise behind us. I turned and saw you, Nancy, standing up with a lit candle in your tiny hand. You were mesmerized by the flame, your eyes glued to its brightness."

Nancy squeezed Violet's fingers tightly, suddenly a little afraid of what their grandfather would say next.

"I called out to you, Nancy, concerned that you would drop the candle. You must have taken alarm at my voice because the candle fell to the floor and rolled onto some of Percival's papers. They quickly caught light, the flames curling and twisting."

"Oh no!" whispered Violet.

A wave of cold skittered up Nancy's back. "What happened next?" she asked nervously, wanting and not wanting to know at the same time.

Grandfather gave Nancy's arm a gentle squeeze. "Agatha called out in alarm, ran to pick you up. The flames raced across the floor, eating the paper as if they had a fearsome hunger. I jumped on the flames, but the fire had taken hold so quickly it had travelled all the way to the window and was already licking at the curtains. I shouted to Agatha to take you outside and I took off my jacket and beat the curtains with it, but it just seemed to fan the flames and give them strength. I realized then that I had to leave, that the cottage was lost."

"It burned down all the way to the ground?" asked Violet.

"It did, Violet. Everything was lost, not one thing inside survived. The three of us stood shivering on the snow-covered grass at the front. Soon flames were licking the roof, and it caught alight too, pieces of the thatch falling to the grass, scorching the ground black."

"Agatha and Percival lost everything," said Nancy, her head spinning with what she had just learned.

"They did," said Grandfather in a low voice. "Agatha insisted that Percival must not know you and I were at the house that day. She said his fury would be too much to bear. She said no matter how the fire had been started, Percival would use it against her. She told me to take you and leave."

Nancy's bottom lip trembled. Grandfather gave her a concerned glance. "I did not want to leave Agatha to face Percival alone, but I also knew that she was right. If he learned of our involvement in the fire, it would make life worse for us all. So, against my better judgement, we left."

Cupola House creaked gently, the window frames rattling in a passing gust of wind. The smell of mint, rosemary and basil drifted under Nancy's nose and she drew in a long, deep breath. She pulled away from her grandfather and wiped at the tears streaking steadily down her cheeks. "It was my fault. I started the fire that sent Agatha to prison."

Grandfather shook his head vehemently and grasped Nancy's hand, pressing all of his warmth into her palm. "No. You were little more than a baby, and it was an accident. This is why the truth has been kept from you, Nancy. We needed to protect you, did not want you to blame yourself."

"Don't cry, Nancy," soothed Violet, patting Nancy's other hand.

Their kindness caused a fresh rush of tears to race

down Nancy's cheeks as the full truth of their family's history sank under her skin.

"Please do not cry, dear girl," said Grandfather, his voice tight with worry. "You must understand that Agatha made the decision to hide the truth and protect us both, so that the mayor had no reason to seek revenge."

"But he got his revenge for losing everything in the cottage fire and not being allowed to have Cupola House anyway," said Nancy miserably, taking the handkerchief Violet passed her and blowing her nose.

"After Agatha was sent to prison, the mayor wrote me the letter – the one he destroyed today. His words made us all realize that if he discovered our involvement in the fire, he would make our lives intolerable. That is why you and your mother left. I missed you both dearly, but all these years I took comfort from the fact that you were both safe," said Grandfather. "Agatha does not blame you for what happened, Nancy. And neither do your mother or I. It is important you understand that."

The events of the day and the new things Nancy had learned about her past spun round in her head like a Catherine wheel. She had a longing for silence to try and order her thoughts. "I think…I need to be on my own," she said, twisting Violet's handkerchief in her fingers.

"My dear, won't you sit for a while longer? We can talk a little more. Was I wrong to think the truth needed to be told?" Grandfather pressed a hand to his lips.

Violet gave their grandfather an anxious glance.

Nancy stood up, her legs feeling unfamiliar and shaky as she walked slowly to her bedroom door. Her mother and Agatha were alone in prison. Time was marching onwards and she could not see how to save them. She felt alone and very scared and wished with her whole heart she could go back in time and had never returned to this town.

CHAPTER 34

Sisters

Nancy curled onto her side in bed, thinking over all she had learned from her grandfather. Until their arrival in Suffolk her life had been ordered, following a routine of predictable school days and weekends with the family she loved. She had a sense that this life was slipping away, like water down a plughole. It had been replaced with something new and unfamiliar and she did not like it one small bit. She thought of the secrets her mother had kept. The grandfather she had never met before this week who was being bullied by the town's mayor. The aunt she hadn't known existed locked in a small damp cell because of a dropped candle. She had no memory of the accident and Grandfather clearly believed it was not her fault, but was that true? She remembered Agatha's soft look when they had met, the way she had held her hands. Perhaps her aunt did not blame her, but it did not make the burden of what had happened any easier to bear and now both Agatha *and* her mother were in prison.

There was a quiet knock at the door. "May I come in?" asked Violet in a small voice. She did not wait for a reply, and the door creaked open. Footsteps padded over to the bed as Nancy continued to stare at the golden birds on the wallpaper. She felt the palm of a small hand on her back. "I've come to see if you're all right," Violet said, the mattress dipping as she sat on the bed.

Nancy swallowed the dryness in her mouth and pushed herself up until she was sitting with her back against the wall. Violet did the same.

"None of this is your fault, Nancy," said Violet, reaching for Nancy's hand. She linked their fingers together, until their palms were joined.

Nancy looked at her younger sister's pink cheeks and glistening eyes. Her wayward hair looked like it hadn't been brushed for days and there was a smear of greasy butter on her dress. But her hand was so warm and so familiar, it was like putting on a favourite glove on a freezing cold day. "Agatha is in prison because of something I did," said Nancy forlornly.

Violet traced a finger over Nancy's knuckles one by one with her free hand, as if she were ascending and descending mountain after tiny mountain. "But it was an accident and not your fault,"

"What about the letter I took from Grandfather that the mayor burned? That was my fault," said Nancy.

"You were just trying to do the right thing," said Violet.

"But everything has gone so wrong, Violet," said Nancy limply. "Father is in Leeds. Mother and Agatha are locked up. Mr Cavendish refuses to speak up."

The cry of the paperboy interrupted her thoughts. Starlings chattered as they flew on warm currents of air outside. The fragrant smell of the herbs drifted in from the landing.

"Maybe *you* should be the one to speak up," said Violet, shifting position on the bed. "*You* should be the one to tell the truth."

"What do you mean?" asked Nancy with a frown.

"Father says telling the truth is the most important thing of all, even if it takes you a while to tell it," said Violet, her voice hopeful.

"That is very sensible advice," said a voice by the door. It was their grandfather carrying a mug of steaming tea. "Marigold for upset and lavender for strength," he said, coming into the room and passing Nancy the mug. She cupped it in her hands, the smell from the infusion soothing her. "You girls have shown nothing but courage since you arrived here. Being away from home, getting to know me, trying to right the wrongs of the past."

Nancy took a sip of tea and thought of her father's everyday quest for the truth as he defended people in court. She thought of her mother's quiet support for the suffragists, and the handkerchiefs she had sewn for Agatha so she could signal to their grandfather. She glanced at Violet's flushed cheeks, her jutting jaw. Putting the mug on the table, she pushed herself off the bed. "The mayor needs to know the truth of what happened the night his cottage burned down: that I started the fire, not Agatha."

Grandfather looked at Nancy with wide eyes. "He would not believe you; it would be our word against his. And how would it help matters?"

"The mayor might not believe us, but isn't it better that he has the full story?" said Nancy, a new determination rooting her feet to the floor. A kernel of an idea was growing inside her brain. "Maybe it is not just the mayor who needs to know the truth."

"What do you mean?" asked their grandfather.

"The mayor has turned the town against you. The townspeople need to learn his true nature," said Nancy. "He's presenting the charity cheque at ten o'clock this evening at the comet party, we heard him telling Mr Cavendish. Everyone in the ballroom will be there to see it. Imagine, Grandfather. We could tell the whole town the truth," she said, her idea unfurling and growing just like the stems of the plants on the landing.

"Yes! The mayor won't be able to ignore us or tell us to go away if lots of people are there," said Violet.

Grandfather smoothed the ends of his moustache, peering at Nancy thoughtfully.

"Mr Cavendish might not be able to stand up to the mayor, but *our* family has been treated unjustly and it is time everyone knew about that. The truth *must* be told," said Nancy firmly.

A flicker of fire seemed to be igniting behind Grandfather's eyes. "I have kept quiet all these years and what good has that done for me? It has only served to make me a prisoner in my own home, afraid to go out." He pulled his shoulders back. "Even if people do not believe us, perhaps it *is* time the truth was told."

CHAPTER 35

Comet Party

Nancy looked to the sky as she followed Violet and their grandfather out of Cupola House a little after nine o'clock that evening. The comet flashed brilliantly, suggesting the form of a glimmering woman with long flowing hair reaching for the stars. It was at its closest point to Earth, yet the air was fresh and sweet. The dire prophecies about the poisonous gas from the comet's tail were false, just as most rational people had predicted.

Grandfather was dressed in the slightly too tight black suit Nancy had found in his wardrobe. Violet had dusted it off, while Nancy had used the ancient flat iron to remove creases from a shirt. They had both helped him attach the collar and cuffs to his shirt and fix the blue silk bow tie round his neck. Violet had pulled the summer dresses their mother had thought to bring from the carpet bag – cream muslin with lace collars and a blue sash for Nancy and a pink sash for Violet. As Nancy laced up her shoes, she had the sudden memory of Mother in her nightgown polishing them a few days before they left for Suffolk. Her throat constricted with worry for their mother alone in her cell.

"No matter what the outcome, we shall all look the picture of respectability tonight," Grandfather said, his eyes glinting with intent as he looked at Nancy and Violet approvingly.

As they strode down Abbeygate Street past the fluttering flags and banners, Nancy noticed the windows above the haberdashery shop were dark; Burch and his parents must already be at the party. She felt a knot of fear and anticipation as they turned the corner at the bottom of the street to find Angel Hill thronging with horse carriages and motor cars that had brought people to the party. The men tending to the horses were busy shovelling up dung or standing in huddles admiring the night sky. Light from the tall Subscription Rooms windows puddled on the pavements, pulling them closer. People chattered excitedly as they queued up on the building's balcony to look at the comet through the brass telescope. Nancy's eyes were drawn upwards to the small copper-domed observatory on the roof. She thought of the money hidden under the floorboards and wished for the hundredth time Mr Cavendish would also do the right thing and stand up to the mayor.

Violet was staring at the pillared entrance to the Rooms, where a lady in a peacock-blue dress and her gentleman companion had been stopped by two suited doormen and were being asked to show their party tickets. "Oh," Violet said in dismay.

"What is it?" asked Nancy.

"We don't have tickets to the party. How will we get inside?" said Violet.

Nancy frowned. Her sister was right. They had overlooked a vital detail in their plan to confront the mayor.

"We are not buying tickets. I refuse to hand over good money only for it to be taken by that thief," said their grandfather gruffly.

"There may be no need," said Nancy, a plan forming in her head. "Burch is at the party. Perhaps we can tell the doormen we have an urgent message for him, and I could slip inside? He'll be happy to help us."

Grandfather frowned. "Hmm. That is not without risk. What if the mayor sees you?"

"I could do it," said Violet, pulling on Nancy's sleeve. "I'm smaller than you and good at hiding."

Nancy shook her head. "No, Violet. It would not be safe."

"Please," said Violet, clasping her hands together and jiggling on the spot. "I want to help."

Nancy and her grandfather exchanged a look. "She is small and nimble. It may be our best chance," said Grandfather.

"I'm as angry as you at the mayor. You must let me help," pleaded Violet. Nancy looked at her little sister's steely jaw, her clenched fists and felt a burst of gratitude and pride. "All right. But you must be careful."

Violet grinned. "Of course."

"There is a tradesmen's entrance to the building on the lane that runs alongside it," said Grandfather, pointing it out. "If you can find Burch, see if he'll take you to it. We'll wait by the door, then you can let us in."

"And don't speak to anyone apart from Burch," said Nancy, taking Violet's hand and giving it a quick squeeze.

With the plan agreed, the three of them approached the front entrance and were greeted by a buzz of noise and activity from within. Through the open doors Nancy saw ladies in fine dresses of lapis, indigo, turquoise and cerulean blue, the sparkle of diamonds and rubies round necks. Gentlemen in dark suits sipped from champagne glasses, their heads tipped back as they joked and laughed. The air crackled with anticipation, like the static before a storm.

Two men were standing near the entrance having a smoke. "Did you hear what Sir Robert Ball of the Cambridge Observatory said about the comet?" said one to the other. "It is as likely that the Empire State Express train from New York to Chicago would run into the night mail train from London to Edinburgh, that the comet would collide head-on with Earth. To think people have even imagined such a thing!" The men roared with laughter. Everyone had pushed any fear of the comet to one side – they were prepared for a night of merriment instead.

The shorter of the two doormen, wearing top hat and

tails, greeted them. "Good evening," he said. "May I see your tickets, please?" He looked at Nancy's grandfather a little harder, his cheeks suddenly tightening. "Mr Greenstone?" He exchanged an uncertain glance with the taller doorman.

Nancy sensed her grandfather stiffen by her side.

"I did not expect to see you here…" the taller doorman said haltingly. "Does the mayor know you are coming?"

Grandfather shook his head. "We are not attending the party. I need to get a message to Burch Cavendish – he is inside."

The doormen looked at one another. "I'm afraid that won't be possible," said the shorter doorman. "Admission is by ticket only."

"And all the tickets have been sold," said the tall doorman.

"My granddaughter, she can take in a message. It is urgent," said Grandfather. The doormen looked at each other again then shook their heads at the same time.

"I know your mother, don't I?" said Grandfather, peering over the top of his spectacles at the tall doorman. "I remember her coming into my shop years ago for a remedy to help her rheumatism. If I recall rightly, the herbs I provided made her feel much improved."

The doorman chewed on his bottom lip, his cheeks flushing.

"Please," said Nancy, looking at Violet. "My sister can deliver the message and be in and out in a flash."

"I'll be ever so quick," said Violet, giving them an innocent wide-eyed look.

The doormen conferred with one another again. "She's just a girl. What harm can come of it?" said the taller one.

"I suppose you're right," said the smaller one, scratching his chin. "Go on then, in you go. You might find Burch helping in the bar upstairs. I saw him heading there a short while ago."

Nancy held her breath as she watched Violet bolt through the entrance door and disappear into the throngs of people.

"Thank you," said Grandfather, giving the doormen a nod. "We shall wait round the corner." Nancy felt the eyes of the two doormen boring into their backs as they nipped round the corner and into the darkness of the lane.

"Violet's inside!" exclaimed Grandfather, his voice

bursting with pride. "I must say, it does feel good to be taking action. It makes me wonder why I have left it so long."

They waited quietly in the shadows by the back door, hearing distant roars of laughter and the clink of glasses. Nancy thought people would not be having quite so much fun if they knew some of the hard-earned money they'd used to buy tickets was lining the mayor's pockets, rather than the charity's.

"Where is she?" asked Nancy after a while. She placed an ear to the door but was greeted by silence. At least five minutes had passed since Violet disappeared inside and she felt a rush of concern for her little sister.

"Have faith," said Grandfather firmly. "I feel sure she will be all right."

Nancy shuffled closer to her grandfather. She had known him for less than a week, yet was fond of him and took comfort from his words.

The sound of the door bolts being drawn back a few minutes later made Nancy jump. The door opened to reveal a small figure and a much taller one illuminated in a blade of light. *Violet and Burch!* Burch's face was as puzzled as a question mark as he stood back and ushered them into a corridor which smelled strongly of steamed fish. Nancy peered at her friend in wonder. His green delivery overalls had been replaced with a grey suit and waistcoat, peach necktie and cream shirt, and his hair was neatly combed. He was a polished version of the boy she had grown to like and admire, a boy who liked learning about science and the stars and went to great lengths to help those in need.

Burch looked at the three of them expectantly. "Mr Greenstone, what are you doing here? Violet found me; she said you needed my help."

"I've told Grandfather everything. We're going to confront the mayor," said Nancy.

Burch's face was a combination of awe and fear. "But what about the threats the mayor made in the observatory this morning? What'll he do to my pa?"

"We'll keep your pa out of it, Burch," said Nancy's grandfather, placing a hand on Burch's shoulder. "He has made his decision to hide the truth and there is nothing we can do about that. But Nancy and Violet have made me realize that it is time the Greenstone family stood up for what is right. I will not cower away any longer with people believing the lies the mayor tells about me and my family. It is time to speak up."

Burch whistled through his teeth. "Gosh, Mr

Greenstone. I've never heard you speak like this before."

There was a cough to their left a little way along the corridor. Nancy turned to see Mr Cavendish's taut cheeks, even paler than usual against his smart dark suit. "Your ma asked me to find you. The mayor's presentation is about to begin," he said to Burch, approaching the four of them warily.

"Hello, Mr Cavendish," said Grandfather in a kind voice, pushing his spectacles onto his nose and blinking.

A flush rose above the collar of Mr Cavendish's necktie. He pulled at it, as if it was too tight. "I heard what you said just now, that you've come to speak up. That's...brave of you."

Mr Greenstone grimaced. "It is not bravery, Mr Cavendish. It is a determination to ensure the truth is told. Whether people choose to believe it will be up to them."

Mr Cavendish fiddled with his cufflinks; his mouth twisted in misery. "In my book telling the truth takes courage, which is something I'm severely lacking." He glanced at Burch. "I know you've a low opinion of me, but I feel trapped by the mayor, on the edge of a precipice."

Burch placed a hand on his father's arm. "Then perhaps it's time to take a leap like Mr Greenstone. Whatever happens, Pa, I'll stand by you."

Mr Cavendish placed a hand over his son's. His stooped shoulders were quivering, just as they had been in the observatory earlier that morning. But instead of staring at the floor and his shoes, he was looking Burch directly in the eyes. "I've wondered many times what would happen if I took control of matters and spoke up about the mayor. Perhaps I was asking myself the wrong question."

"What do you mean?" asked Burch.

Mr Cavendish's Adam's apple bobbed in his throat. "I should've thought about what would happen if I didn't stand up to the mayor – and the answer's a life under his thumb, and I can't bear any more of that."

A slow dawn was rising in Burch's eyes. "You'll speak up too then, tell the truth?"

Mr Cavendish gave Mr Greenstone and the children a small and shaky smile. "Mayor Douglas's actions have throttled me for far too long. I need to cut the noose, no matter what the outcome."

"Yes," hissed Violet.

Mr Cavendish looked at her and smiled softly,

shaking his head a little. "These children have taught us a thing or two about standing up for the truth."

"Indeed," said their grandfather, patting Mr Cavendish on the back. "We are stronger in numbers, Mr Cavendish. I am proud of your decision and I will stand by you too, no matter what happens this evening."

"We need to go," said Nancy, hearing voices at the end of the corridor.

"Yes, folks were already gathering in the ballroom when I came looking for Burch," said Mr Cavendish. He turned to Burch and Violet. "If I'm going to speak up, I need to do it well. Would the two of you be able to help me with something?"

"Of course," said Violet.

"Absolutely," said Burch with a grin.

"Good," said Mr Cavendish. His shoulders seemed to be lengthening and straightening before Nancy's eyes now he had decided to take action. "Two beats of the gong will announce the mayor's presentation of the charity cheque from the balcony," he said. "The mayor will come up the main stairs to make a grand entrance, so it will be safe to wait in the corridor that adjoins the balcony. I'll be as quick as I can with Violet and Burch."

A combination of nerves and excitement knotted Nancy's stomach. She thought of her father representing clients in court, how he'd told her that in his early days he had to fight his nerves by pushing all other thoughts from his head and focusing on the message he needed to deliver. Nancy's message was clear as a bell in her mind. This was about telling the truth and clearing Mother's and Agatha's names. But how would the mayor and the people of the town react to hearing what they had to say? Would they be booed and hissed from the ballroom? Would the mayor have them ushered away by the police? A loud boom vibrated in Nancy's ears. It was the first gong! The mayor's speech was about to begin.

CHAPTER 36

Doing the Right Thing

Light from the sparkling chandeliers, the pop of champagne corks and the musky smell of perfume greeted Nancy and her grandfather as they waited in the corridor behind the balcony from where the mayor was about to make his speech.

Nancy glanced at her grandfather, noticing the crevices in his brow. He pulled his handkerchief from his pocket, took off his spectacles for a moment and dabbed at the beads of sweat on his forehead. She reached across and placed a hand on his arm. He gave her a shaky smile and pushed the handkerchief back into his pocket.

"Three cheers for the mayor," shouted a voice, louder than all the rest.

A round of thunderous applause, whistles and whoops made Grandfather's eyes widen with alarm. How had the mayor hoodwinked the people at this party into liking and respecting him? He had confronted her grandfather, belittled him and made him fearful. It must be taking every ounce of his courage to be standing beside her now, about to stand up to him. Nancy thought of her mother's support for women campaigning together to have a vote and a voice. She thought of her father's constant fight for truth and justice in the legal system. "This is the right thing to do. We can do this together," Nancy whispered firmly.

Her grandfather gave her a wobbly nod.

"Thank you so much, my honourable ladies and gentlemen." The mayor's silken voice curled round the corner and Nancy felt her grandfather bristle by her side.

"As you know," began the mayor, "this party to celebrate the historic passing of Halley's comet has been many months in the planning and it will raise much-needed money for charitable causes."

Heat was spreading up from Nancy's toes, flashing

up her legs and climbing up her back as she listened to the mayor's false promises.

"It will be another seventy-six years before this comet passes by Earth again, something that will be witnessed by your children and grandchildren. It is, however, lucky that I am here today at all, to witness the passing of this comet and present this cheque to charity, following an attempt made on my life only the other evening."

Nancy heard gasps and mutters coming from the ballroom below. The mayor had paused, was sucking up the town's sympathy like a delicious drink through a paper straw. She wiped her palms on her dress and glanced behind for Burch, Violet and Mr Cavendish, but they were nowhere to be seen. Could Mr Cavendish have had a change of heart?

"So, without further ado, let me present this cheque for the sum of…"

"Are you ready?" Nancy asked her grandfather, taking his hand, her legs feeling like rubber.

"Yes," he whispered.

Nancy took a deep and steadying breath, her pulse whooshing loudly in her ears. They rushed round the corner and onto the balcony boldly, as if they were running into the sea on a winter's day.

Nancy blinked at the sight of the chandeliers that were throwing dazzling beads of light onto the brass telescopes lined up beneath the huge windows. She blinked again at the heads bobbing below, necks tilted, all eyes focused on the mayor as he held up the charity cheque. Another blink as she took in the mayor's red ceremonial robes, the gold chain of office glimmering over his black dinner suit. An aura of power and control surrounded him as Nancy and her grandfather walked towards the balustrade and the eyes of the town slipped away from the mayor and settled on them instead. Murmurs and whispers accompanied the eyes.

"Is that Mr Greenstone?"

"Who's that young girl with him?"

"What are they doing up there with the mayor?"

The mayor's smile began to wane as he watched the townspeople whisper and point.

Grandfather gave Nancy's hand a final squeeze and then dropped it. He leaned against the balustrade and gripped the handrail. "Good evening," he said. His voice was weak, barely audible.

The mayor swivelled, his jaw dropping as he saw Nancy and her grandfather. "What...why..." he blustered, looking around for help. "Leave this balcony immediately," he demanded in a low voice.

The people in the ballroom below had quietened, and were listening eagerly. Nancy saw one woman take a seat and lean forward; her eyes glued to the unfolding drama as if she were watching a play at the theatre.

"No. My granddaughter and I are not going anywhere," said Grandfather, his voice a little stronger now. "Ladies and gentlemen, if I could have a minute of your time, there are some matters I must speak of…"

"Go! Now!" said the mayor through gritted teeth, lunging for Grandfather's arm.

Nancy felt a tremor in her breastbone as she watched her grandfather shrug him off and continue to speak.

"For many years I have been living alone in Cupola House, afraid of Mayor Douglas. He has told lies about my business, turned people against me, caused me to send my family away in fear of what he may do to them," Grandfather said, his voice now loud and clear.

More whispers and gasps of disbelief from the ballroom.

"Mr Greenstone," said the mayor, reaching again for his arm. "If you do not leave this instant I shall have you forcibly removed." He looked over the balcony.

"Is Constable Addison here?" he called. "I am in need of assistance."

As the two men began to scuffle and the audience's mutters grew louder, Nancy saw the constable she had met at the police station spring to his feet and make his way to the stairs. She glanced behind for Violet and the others but there was still no sign of them. Her chin trembled. She had to help her grandfather before their opportunity to confront the mayor was brought to a halt. Stepping forward she gripped the handrail too, as she glanced at the constable advancing up the stairs. She turned her attention to the people below. "Um… excuse me. My grandfather is trying to tell you something," she said. Her voice was mouse-small, and everyone's attention was focused on the continuing scuffle. Nancy drew in a breath. Then another. The constable was almost at the top of the stairs. "Will you please listen!" she shouted across the ballroom.

The chatter and whispers silenced, as if smothered by a heavy blanket. The constable paused and looked at Nancy quizzically. The mayor and her grandfather stopped grappling for a moment and were staring at her too. Hundreds of pairs of eyes focused on Nancy, hands clapped to mouths, shared looks of disbelief passing between the crowd like falling dominoes.

Nancy's legs shook as she stared into the crowd, her gaze settling on Mrs Cavendish. Her hands were clasped in front of her pale grey silk dress, embroidered butterflies fluttering around the neckline. Her eyes were bright, and she gave Nancy an encouraging nod. The attention steadied her, like a rocking chair being stilled. "My grandfather is right, the mayor is a liar," Nancy said, forcing all of her strength into her voice.

Gasps and shakes of heads from the ballroom below.

Nancy ignored them and glanced at her grandfather. *Do the right thing. She must do the right thing.* "Mayor Douglas has treated my grandfather terribly because he changed his will so the mayor would not inherit Cupola House. He has been trying to get revenge on my family ever since and has put both my mother and aunt – his own wife – in prison."

There were further gasps and whispers as ripples of shock passed around the people in the ballroom.

Nancy's words seemed to jolt the now purple-faced mayor into action. "Constable Addison! Remove. These. People. From. The. Balcony!"

Constable Addison had advanced to the top of the stairs. "Hang on a minute, I know you," he said, pointing at Nancy. "You were enquiring at the police station about the woman who tried to burn down the mayor's house. Are you telling me she's your mother?"

"Yes," said Nancy, turning to look over the crowd below. "But she didn't start the fire at the mayor's house…" She paused and glanced back while the crowd chattered excitedly, her eyes searching for Mr Cavendish, who would be able to confirm the truth of what had happened that night. But with dismay, she saw there was still no sign of him, Burch or Violet. What was keeping them?

"What my granddaughter says is true," called Grandfather, finally twisting free from the mayor's grasp and rushing to Nancy's side. "I also wish people to know that the fire which destroyed the mayor's cottage ten years ago was not caused by my daughter Agatha. It was an accident, yet she has been blamed for it all these years." He lowered his head a little. "The mayor does not like people talking about these events, or his wife, and I am ashamed to say that I was afraid to speak up because of the threats he made against my family."

The mayor's laugh was as hard as granite. "Lies, all lies," he said, opening his arms wide. "Agatha deliberately burned my cottage to the ground and caused me to lose everything I own."

A white-hot rage roared through Nancy, spots dancing in front of her eyes. "No," she cried out. "It was not Agatha's fault. The truth is that I was there. I was only small but I dropped a candle. I accidentally started the fire that destroyed your cottage. Agatha took the blame to protect me."

The mayor's eyes widened. He began to splutter and pull at his gold chain as if it was a lead weight pulling him down.

Silence crept across the ballroom, the mutters and gasps dying away as the crowd absorbed Nancy's words.

The mayor's face became mottled purple and pink as he stared at Nancy, his eyes blinking furiously. "For the last time, Constable Addison, arrest these people at once!"

CHAPTER 37

Speaking Up

Constable Addison sprang up the final few steps and placed a hand on Grandfather's arm. "Don't make a fuss, Mr Greenstone. You will only make things worse for yourself and your family," he said in a low voice.

Nancy looked at the constable with alarm, her faith in the idea that they could resolve everything slamming into the floor.

"I don't know what you were thinking, bringing your personal business here to the mayor's party," Constable Addison continued.

"But people need to know the truth," said Nancy, balling her clammy hands into fists. She looked with dismay at the crowd in the ballroom, now discussing the events loudly. Then from the corner of her eye she noticed a pink-cheeked Mrs Cavendish bring a hand to her throat, her eyes focusing on something behind Nancy's head. Nancy whipped round to see Violet, Burch and Mr Cavendish rushing onto the balcony carrying the metal cash boxes. *They had been taking up the floorboards in the observatory.*

"Constable Addison. Please let go of Mr Greenstone. There's something I have to say too," said Mr Cavendish. With his shoulders pulled back and his head held high he towered over them all.

The mayor looked at Mr Cavendish, then at the cash boxes, his mottled cheeks suddenly paling. "Put. Those. Back," he hissed, waving his chauffeur away.

Nancy saw Mr Cavendish waver for a moment, and she held her breath, hoping he would keep his newly found courage and still speak up. Thankfully Mr Cavendish ignored the mayor's instruction, strode to the balustrade and looked over the crowd. Nancy exhaled slowly.

"What Mr Greenstone and his granddaughter have

just told you is the truth. I've had the same treatment from Mayor Douglas; bullying and threats to my business and family. The mayor forced me to lie, to say that I'd seen Charlotte Greenstone start the fire at his house on Monday night, when it was him who started it. I'm truly sorry for that and am prepared to face the consequences."

Mutters and gasps of disbelief whirled over the balcony.

The mayor gave Mr Cavendish a withering look.

Mr Cavendish looked down on the mayor as if he were a slug chewing on salad leaves.

"More lies!" barked the mayor. He looked to Constable Addison, who had released Grandfather's arm and was now watching the mayor through narrowed eyes.

Nancy thought that for someone so powerful, the mayor was not doing a very good job of defending himself. Perhaps that was because, really, there was nothing he could say to defend his dastardly actions.

There was a call from below, a hand waving in the air. It was Mr Thompson the wine merchant. He started to speak but could not be heard above the chaotic din.

"Quiet," called Mr Cavendish.

"Let the man speak," called Grandfather.

Burch put two fingers in his mouth and whistled loudly.

The crowd slowly silenced. Mr Thompson gave a grateful nod and began again. "I believe everything Mr Cavendish and Mr Greenstone have said here tonight," he began, his cheeks flushed. "Mayor Douglas makes me supply wine for all of his parties for nothing, threatening he will tell folks my drink is sour as vinegar if I don't."

Nancy gasped.

Another hand raised. "It's Mr Collins the fishmonger," Nancy heard her grandfather say, gripping the handrail.

"Mayor Douglas has threatened me too. He said if I didn't give him free seafood, he would tell people my fish was off, and that they should shop elsewhere," shouted Mr Collins.

That was why the two men had sounded so bitter about the fine food and wine they were supplying to the party – the mayor was forcing them to provide their goods for free so he could keep more of the profits.

Another hand raised and another and another. Nancy listened in amazement as the voices of shopkeepers, innkeepers and tradesmen chimed across the ballroom, telling tales of how the mayor had bullied and threatened them and instructed them to have nothing to do with Mr Greenstone or his apothecary shop.

"Well I never," said Nancy's grandfather, shaking his head. "The mayor has tried to threaten and squash us all, and not one of us has had the courage to speak up until now."

Constable Addison looked at the mayor suspiciously. "Is there any truth to these claims, Percival?"

"Of course not!" blustered the mayor, his purple cheeks clashing horribly with his crimson robes. A sheen of sweat glistened on his forehead.

"There's more," called Mr Cavendish, holding up a cash box. "The mayor threatened me because I discovered he'd been stealing some of the ticket money from his charity parties and keeping it for himself."

Nancy watched as Mr Cavendish placed the two cash boxes he was holding on the floor, opened one and pulled out a sheaf of banknotes. He held them up for the crowd to see. Violet and Burch did the same and Nancy felt a glow of pride at their determination to help.

Constable Addison marched over to the open cash box at Burch's feet and examined the contents. He whistled through his teeth. "There's enough money here to open a small bank," he said, glancing back at the mayor, whose whole body was trembling as if he had been plunged into a lake of ice-cold water.

"Stop!" called Nancy, waving her hands as the crowd talked wildly amongst themselves. There was a question she was desperate to ask the mayor, but it was impossible to make herself heard. She glanced at the large brass gong standing against the wall at the back of the balcony. Violet must have been following her gaze, for she dropped the banknotes she was holding into the cash box and ran over to the gong, picked up the beater and hit it with all of her might. The sound vibrated around the ballroom, silencing people once more.

"Why did you do it?" asked Nancy, taking a step towards the mayor. "I know you tried to get revenge on my family, but why treat everyone else so horribly, stealing from them and threatening them? And why hide the money in the town observatory?"

The mayor looked at Nancy aghast, spluttering out a laugh. "You are just a child. I am the mayor of this town and I don't have to answer to anyone."

"Oh, but I think you do, Percival," said Constable Addison, who was now hovering at Nancy's side. "In fact, it seems this girl is your niece. She deserves an explanation and I would very much like to hear it too."

The mayor rubbed at his neck and looked over the crowd. His shoulders dipped a little and he turned back to look at Nancy and her grandfather, his lips set in a cruel, hard line. "You dare to come here and confront me at my party to celebrate the passing of the comet."

"You don't even like the comet," called out Burch, his cheeks taut. "You're afraid of it, tried to buy anti-comet pills from every chemist in town. You only held this party because you saw a way of making money from it."

The mayor looked at Burch thinly. "Who wouldn't be fearful of a gaseous star hurtling towards Earth?"

Burch's incredulous bell-like laugh rang around the ballroom. "The comet isn't a star. It has a nucleus of ice, rock and dust. You don't know the first thing about objects in the night sky, do you?"

Mr Cavendish looked at his son with wonder, his cheeks puffing with pride.

But Burch's words flared the mayor's anger, his heavy chain quivering like a twisted golden snake round his neck. "How dare you mock and belittle me? I lost the magnificent house and cupola I should have rightly inherited. My cottage burned to the ground destroying my possessions. Everyone knows that it is wealth and property that makes a person powerful."

Like another beat of the gong Nancy realized something. "Everything you did…the lies and the threats and the stealing, even hiding the money up high in the observatory. It was all about being powerful?" she said incredulously.

"I was elected mayor; being powerful and above everyone else is what is expected of me," said the mayor, as if this was a perfectly acceptable explanation.

"No, you are wrong," said Nancy, her voice cracking with pent-up anger. "Doing the right thing with your power is what people expected of you."

"Quite right," said Constable Addison, giving Nancy an appraising look.

"Absolutely," said Nancy's grandfather, clasping his hands together.

"It seems we might also need to investigate how you've remained mayor for so many years, Percival. If it also involved threatening the good people of this town perhaps they will now feel able to speak up too," said the constable.

Nancy saw a few nods and exchanges of looks from

people in the crowd below as the constable reached into his jacket pocket and pulled out a pair of handcuffs. The mayor saw this too and his eyes were suddenly like those of a frightened rabbit. In a lightning-swift move, the mayor ran towards Violet, his eyes fixed on the cash boxes by her shoes.

"No!" cried Nancy, lunging towards her little sister, but Violet had also understood the mayor's intentions and she quickly opened the boxes, scooped up the banknotes and ran to the balustrade. She hurled the notes over the edge, money raining down on the ballroom like paper snow.

"No," called the mayor in anguish, as Burch and his father gathered handfuls of banknotes and did the same.

Throwing Constable Addison a desperate look, the mayor ran down the stairs to the ballroom, his robes falling from his shoulders, his gold chain clanking, his feet slipping and sliding in his hurry.

Constable Addison was close on his heels.

"Stop him!" called Nancy, grabbing Violet's hand and leaning over the balustrade. She saw the crowd were watching in silent shock as the purple-faced mayor pushed people aside in his desperate bid to escape.

Nancy and Violet exchanged a quick look and then bolted for the stairs, Burch following close behind.

"Come back, girls!" cried their grandfather, but Nancy ignored him.

The mayor barged across the ballroom like a bulldog, pushing past every obstacle in his way. He overturned chairs and bumped into tables, knocked a man to the ground who dared to try and block his path.

"The mayor's trying to leave by the back door to the ballroom. We might cut him off if we go the other way," cried Burch, as they reached the bottom of the stairs.

The crowd had become raucous again, as they watched the back of the retreating mayor, with Constable Addison in pursuit. Glasses of champagne and dinner plates wobbled from tables and shattered on the floor, as the two men pushed onwards.

Nancy clenched Violet's hand so tightly she was afraid it would break, as they ran through the double doors under the balcony and into the entrance hall. The front doors were wide open and a cool breeze rushed in to greet them. The doormen were nowhere to be seen, perhaps lured into the ballroom by the commotion.

"What now?" gasped Violet.

They could hear cries from the ballroom and heavy

footsteps through another doorway; the mayor and Constable Addison were approaching.

"The balloons!" said Nancy, noticing the two strings holding the comet balloon arrangement in place either side of the door. "If they fall they might be a distraction."

"Yes! You pull one string, I'll pull the other," said Burch to Nancy, running to the other side of the doorway.

Nancy pulled down hard on her string, and the balloons bumped and wobbled. She yanked harder and one side of the balloon arrangement loosened but did not fall.

Burch pulled on the other string but it held taut. "It's stuck," he said through gritted teeth.

Violet dashed across to Burch. "Let me help," she cried.

Nancy caught a glimpse of the mayor's red robes through the doorway and heard the constable's raspy breaths as he chased after him.

Burch and Violet pulled down hard on the other string and it snapped just as the mayor ran through the door. He looked up in confusion, his hands automatically shooting up to shield his head as the silver balloons rained down on him.

It was a long enough pause for Constable Addison to clamp a heavy hand on the mayor's shoulder. "That… is…enough…Percival. You are embarrassing yourself," wheezed the constable.

"You certainly are," said Burch's father, who rushed in from behind to block the mayor's path.

Mayor Douglas's shoulders stooped and his eyes dulled as he realized the chase was over. Giving the children one last withering look, he dropped to the floor, the folds of his cloak and the silver comet balloons enveloping him as he let out an anguished moan.

Nancy lowered her gaze. She was glad the mayor would finally get his comeuppance, but it didn't feel right to watch his distress. She turned away and strode over to Burch and Violet.

"We stopped him," said Burch in delight.

"We did it!" said Violet, her eyes sparkling.

But Nancy had been distracted by a man in a beige mackintosh carrying a small travelling bag. He had just walked through the front entrance and was looking at the events in bewilderment. She blinked, her heart soaring. "Look," she said to Violet, pointing.

"Father!" said Violet, dashing towards him.

Nancy's grandfather was out of breath from rushing

down the stairs to join them. He put an arm around Nancy's shoulders. "Is that him? Is that your father, Jacob?" he asked, seeming quite unsurprised to see him there.

"Yes. But how…" began Nancy.

"Your mother gave me the telephone number of his solicitors' office, with the strict instructions only to use it in a dire emergency. This seemed like one, so I placed a call at the post office this morning after breakfast. Your father said he would take the first train to Suffolk, arriving here this evening. I didn't tell you in case he ran into difficulties and your hopes were dashed," said Grandfather, his smile the widest Nancy had ever seen it.

Nancy ran towards her father, hope and love springing her forward. Violet clung to his arm like a limpet and he folded them both into a hug. Nancy smelled the tang of train oil, long journeys and a hint of Monty the terrier.

"My darling girls. Whatever has happened?" he said. "Your mother sets off for Suffolk leaving only the vaguest of messages. I arrive at Cupola House, follow the note on the shop door sending me here to find complete pandemonium."

Nancy looked up at her father's anxious eyes and

dishevelled hair. "It's a long story," she said, glancing at her grandfather, who was still smiling and dabbing at his watery eyes with his handkerchief.

"Then you had better start at the beginning," her father said, hugging her and Violet so close that Nancy ached, but in a very good way indeed.

CHAPTER 38

Goodbye and Hello

The morning after the comet party, Agatha and Charlotte said goodbye to their prison cells while the mayor said hello to his. Nancy's family stood in a tight huddle of reunion in the apothecary shop, the jars and bottles glinting in the sunlight that spilled through the open blinds.

"You are so brave and a credit to this family, girls," their mother said. She bit on her lip and glanced at her own sister. Her face crumpled like one of the handkerchiefs they had sewn.

"I was most alarmed to receive the telephone call

from Mr Greenstone at my solicitors' office. Didn't know what to think," said their father, who had gone to the prison with Constable Addison to secure the release of their mother and aunt.

"I am so sorry I felt unable to tell you the truth of my family's history, my darling," said their mother, grasping their father's hands. "We met and married so quickly, and knowing of your profession, I feared you would think badly of me, if you discovered I had a sister in prison. As time went by, I desperately wanted to tell you the truth, but could never summon the courage to do so, fearing what you would think of us and what the mayor might do if he found out."

"I would have helped you, Charlotte," said Nancy's father sadly.

"I realize that now," said their mother, her eyes filling with tears.

"Oh, don't cry," beseeched their father, embracing her. "I am worried by these events, of course, but the important thing is the truth has been told," he said, glancing at Nancy's grandfather and Agatha, who were also entwined in an embrace. "I think a good solicitor is needed to advise Agatha on the termination of her marriage to the mayor. I can certainly help with that."

"Thank you, my dear. I have loved Agatha fiercely all of my life, and I would do anything to protect her and my family," said their mother.

"A sister's love is like no other," said Agatha, as she looked at Nancy's mother, wiping the tears from her cheeks with a red-edged handkerchief.

Nancy glanced at Violet, who was sitting on the countertop, smiling in wonderment at the happy family reunion. She had grown to know her little sister well these past few days and felt proud of her courage and grit. They were bound to disagree on things as time marched on, squabble and fall out. But beneath it all she realized that Agatha was right; a sister's love really was like no other.

That afternoon, Nancy trailed behind Agatha and her grandfather, as they roamed Cupola House from bottom to top, Agatha greeting every potted herb, every dust-sheeted room and object with a smile of pure joy that was tinged with an edge of sadness. In Nancy's attic bedroom Agatha picked up the embroidered pillowslip and held it to her chest. "I loved looking after you when you were small. It saddens me that we have been apart so many years."

"I wish it could have been different," said Nancy, suddenly feeling shy.

Agatha returned the pillow to the cot and walked over to Nancy hesitantly. "I suppose all that matters now is that we are able to make new memories – together." She tipped Nancy's chin and peered at her with bright eyes. "Knocking over the candle which destroyed the cottage was an accident, you must think no more of it."

"But aren't you angry, being locked away for all those years for something you did not do?" asked Nancy, a small burn in the base of her throat.

Agatha let her hand fall to her side and shook her head. "Anger is a wasted emotion. Percival took everything from me, but I was determined the one thing he wouldn't do was break my spirit. I had many years to think in prison and I decided that if I was freed, I would try and put my remaining years to good use. I feel certain I can do that with my family around me." Agatha gave Nancy a tentative hug and she breathed in the smell of lavender water, the last of the tension in her shoulders finally melting away.

After Nancy and Violet had gone to bed that evening, their mother and father came to sit with them for a while.

"Hearing how you confronted the mayor so clearly and eloquently – we wonder if you both might follow in my footsteps and study law?" said their father.

"But women aren't allowed to be solicitors," Nancy said with a frown.

"Not yet," admitted their father, "but times are changing quickly. It seems wholly unfair that you or Violet could not pursue the career you wish just because you are women. I shall be joining your mother and petitioning the government for change."

"Quite right," said their mother. "Perhaps, Nancy, you would like to accompany me when I next go to a meeting of the local suffrage society? I think you would make a fine campaigner and have much to contribute."

"Can I come too?" asked Violet hopefully.

Their mother smiled. "When you are a little older. Just concentrate on sewing handkerchiefs to support the cause for now."

Violet clapped a hand to her forehead and groaned, and they all smiled.

"There is one thing I would like to know," Nancy said, looking at her mother. "What made you decide to return to Cupola House now?"

"It was the comet," her mother said simply. "It is

travelling so fast and resurfaced memories of Agatha's arrest. It made me think of all the years ahead that I would need to keep the truth from you, Violet and your father. I wrote to the mayor frequently, begging him to release Agatha from prison. But it never made any difference. When I heard your grandfather had not seen Agatha's signal from the prison yard for a while and was concerned for her safety, I decided I must risk returning here to resolve matters. But Percival was so intent on seeking revenge he tried to silence me." She smiled at Nancy. "It seems he badly underestimated my family. I don't approve of all of your antics, and the tale of your prison escapade still makes me feel a little faint, but it was you, Nancy – and Violet and Burch – and your resolve to help that has brought my family together again and for that I'm grateful."

Nancy felt her cheeks crease into a grin as she looked at her mother, father and sister. It was hard to believe that yesterday things had seemed so hopeless and yet now here they all were, together again.

"Would you like me to read you a story?" their father asked Violet, kissing her goodnight.

"Um, I was wondering if Nancy might?" she replied.

"Of course," said Nancy, climbing out of her bed

and into her sister's, their parents looking on in surprise.

"It seems there have been some other changes while you have been away from home," said their father, his voice a little bemused.

"Good changes I think," said Nancy, smiling at her sister.

"Very good changes indeed," agreed Violet happily.

In the cupola the following night, Nancy smoothed a hand over the velvet bench-cushion as she watched Burch gaze through her grandfather's telescope.

"The comet's dimmer than it was two nights ago. Mr Watts says that's because it's moved further from the sun," said Burch.

Violet took a sip of warm cocoa, then a large bite from a slice of bread and raspberry conserve their mother had brought upstairs to fuel their night watching. "I wonder if the mayor has a view of the comet from his prison cell," she said through sticky lips.

Nancy thought back over the events of the past two days. The mayor was going on trial for alleged theft and intimidation and in the weeks to come would have to stand in the dock and defend himself, for it seemed no solicitors in the town were prepared to represent him. Her father said he was likely to be in prison for many years to come.

"How is your father?" Nancy asked Burch, as her friend stood back to allow Violet to look through the telescope.

"He's unlikely to face criminal charges, but Ma and I'll be there for him whatever the outcome," said Burch. "Ma's baking currant buns all hours of the day and night for those who stood up to the mayor at the party and all the stolen money has been given to charity."

"Quite right," said Violet, her eye glued to the view of the comet.

"Grandfather's shop has never been so busy, and he's put all of his herbs outside again," said Nancy. "Agatha is determined to make a good life for herself, says she will help him run the shop, and they plan to renovate the house eventually and get electricity and a flushing toilet. Mother says we can come and stay here often, perhaps even for the summer holidays."

"So we'll see each other again," said Burch, grinning. "Speaking of school, Mr Watts has said he'll speak with Ma and Pa about me going to the boys' grammar.

He says I've a talent for science and working out problems."

"I'd say he is right there," said Nancy with a smile, pleased that her friend was another step closer to achieving his ambitions. "Perhaps you will make discoveries about comets and planets, learn new things we couldn't even imagine to be true."

"I'd like that," said Burch, his grin widening. "Mr Watts also says we'll be able to see Halley's comet through a telescope for another year. I'm hoping we'll be able to look at it through the big telescope at the town observatory, now we know it isn't broken."

"Imagine the view through that," said Nancy with a smile.

"You should have a look through Grandfather's telescope now, Nancy," urged Violet.

Nancy finished her cocoa, took the telescope from her sister and readjusted the focus until the comet grew clear. Burch was right, the glowing nucleus and tail were fainter. The comet had burst into their lives, pulling them along with it and opening all of their eyes to lies and hardships that had finally been overcome with courage and the truth. She looked away from the metal eyepiece and glanced at Burch and Violet tucking into the remaining slices of bread. Their lives were not like the ever-returning comet: they were likely to travel on very different paths. But they all shared a strong desire to do the right thing. It was what had caused them to be sitting together watching the comet in this small rooftop cupola, and at that moment Nancy could not wish to be anywhere, or with anyone, else.

My inspiration behind writing
Mystery of the Night Watchers

The first seed of an idea for this story arose from an article I read about Halley's comet, named after the seventeenth century British astronomer Edmond Halley. The orbit of Halley's comet makes it visible from Earth on average every seventy-five to seventy-six years, and when I began to research its appearance in 1910, I discovered that some members of the scientific community at that time thought that the gas present in the comet's tail could poison the air we breathe. I read many old newspaper articles and learned that this hysteria was felt in many parts of the world. All of the things I refer to in the book did happen, such as the manufacture of anti-comet pills by people trying to make some easy money, the sale of gas masks and the advice to seal up windows and doors. But, as we now know from further scientific research, this gas was not a threat and the comet blazed past Earth without incident, with many more people choosing to celebrate it instead. It was these conflicting views of fear and joy at the comet's arrival that I wanted to convey in Nancy's story. Halley's comet was last seen in 1986, and will next return in 2061, so get your telescopes ready for what is likely to be a spectacle you won't want to miss!

Once I'd decided to write about Halley's comet, I needed a worthy building where someone might view it from. The magnificent seventeenth-century Cupola House is an iconic landmark in my hometown of Bury St Edmunds in Suffolk and fitted the bill perfectly. I've gazed up at the house's vaulted cupola, a type of rooftop observatory, countless times, wondering who might have sat up there and taken in the bird's-eye view. There isn't enough space here to cover the building's fascinating history (which includes a devastating fire in 2012 and its subsequent restoration), but I can tell you that it was originally owned by a prosperous apothecary which inspired Nancy's grandfather's shop in the story. When the current restaurant occupiers of the building very kindly offered to give me a tour, I jumped for joy! As I stood inside the cupola and looked over the roofs of Bury, along streets and even into other people's homes, my book idea began to form more clearly. What if the family in my story were pretending to look through their telescope at the comet, but were in fact looking at something else? What if something had happened at the town prison? But here I had a problem, because the town prison in 1910 wouldn't have been visible from the cupola. However, I reminded myself that I was telling a story so I took a dollop of artistic licence and moved my fictional prison closer to the centre of the town, as seen on the map at the front of the book. While Cavendish's Haberdashery is also fictional, the other shops I refer to in the book did exist, and Thurlow Champness Jewellers at 14 Abbeygate Street is still trading today.

As I plotted my first draft, I spent many hours wandering around Bury St Edmunds mapping out where my characters might have walked as they tried to solve the unwinding mystery of the night watchers. If you ever find yourself in Bury St Edmunds, you too can follow the same paths that I did – and that Nancy and Violet walk in the story. On one of these walks, I passed the Subscription Rooms, now known as The Athenaeum, which was built in the 1850s for social occasions and meetings (Charles Dickens gave a six-chapter reading of *David Copperfield* there in 1861!). Perhaps because I'd been writing about telescopes and comets, I noticed for the first time on its roof a small green dome. My heart leaped in my chest. Could it be an observatory? To my utter amazement, I learned about what has been described as "an almost unique Victorian astronomy time capsule" (Astronomy historian, Dr Allan Chapman, Wadham College, Oxford). It is thought that Donati's comet, which passed close to the Earth in 1858, captured the interest of the local scientific community in Bury St Edmunds and prompted the building of the observatory and installation of a large telescope that is still there today. For safety reasons, the observatory sadly isn't open to the public, but there is an ongoing campaign to restore the structure and encourage its educational use.

I hope you enjoyed reading about my inspiration for *Mystery of The Night Watchers*. Perhaps next time you walk along a street, or peer up at the night sky, you will also see something that will spark an idea for a story. Inspiration for stories can be found everywhere, you just need to keep your eyes open and let your imagination run wild!

USBORNE QUICKLINKS

For links to websites where you can see photos of Halley's comet, and find out more about everyday life in the Edwardian era with newsreels of people, places and events, go to usborne.com/Quicklinks and type in the title of this book.

At Usborne Quicklinks you can:

- Browse photos of Halley's comet taken in 1910
- See inside the Athenaeum Observatory in Bury St Edmunds
- Watch film footage of Edwardians enjoying days out
- See women protesting peacefully for the right to vote
- Watch a newsreel of the funeral of King Edward VII

Please follow the internet safety guidelines at Usborne Quicklinks. Children should be supervised online.

The websites recommended at Usborne Quicklinks are regularly reviewed but Usborne Publishing is not responsible and does not accept liability for the availability or content of any website other than its own, or for any exposure to harmful, offensive or inaccurate material which may appear on the Web. Usborne Publishing will have no liability for any damage or loss caused by viruses that may be downloaded as a result of browsing the sites it recommends.

DISCOVER MORE HEART-POUNDING HISTORICAL MYSTERIES FROM A.M. HOWELL…

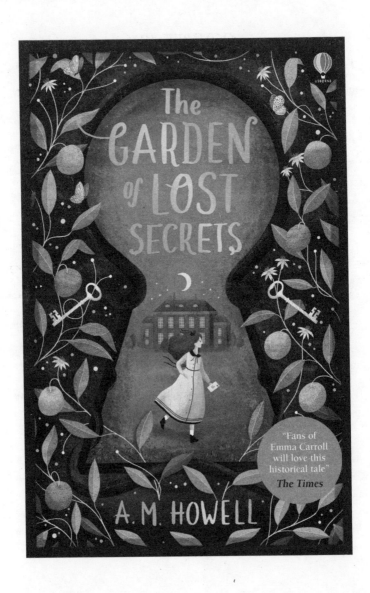

OCTOBER, 1916.

Clara has been sent to stay with her aunt and uncle while England is at war. But when she reaches their cottage on an enormous country estate, Clara is plunged into a tangle of secrets... A dark, locked room, a scheming thief, and a mysterious boy who only appears at night.

Clara has a secret of her own too – a terrible one about her brother, fighting in the war. And as the secrets turn to danger, Clara must find the courage to save herself, and those around her...

"Fans of Emma Carroll will adore this historical tale of derring-do and righted wrongs." *The Times, Children's Book of the Week*

The
HOUSE
of
ONE HUNDRED
CLOCKS

A. M. HOWELL

The critically-acclaimed author of **The Garden of Lost Secrets**

JUNE, 1905.

Helena and her parrot, Orbit, are swept off to Cambridge when her father is appointed clock-winder to one of the wealthiest men in England. There is only one rule: the clocks must never stop.

Soon Helena discovers the house of one hundred clocks holds many mysteries; a ghostly figure, strange notes and stolen winding keys… Can she work out the house's secrets before time runs out?

**WINNER OF THE MAL PEET CHILDREN'S AWARD
WINNER OF THE EAST ANGLIAN BOOK OF
THE YEAR**

"Howell is a hypnotically readable writer, who keeps the pulse racing, while allowing every character slowly to unravel." *The Telegraph*

AND LOOK OUT FOR
FURTHER GRIPPING
HISTORICAL MYSTERIES
FROM A.M. HOWELL,
COMING IN 2022...

Acknowledgements

Just as the first 2020 pandemic lockdown began I realized, with a rising panic, I had taken some wrong turns with the plot of this story. But thankfully my fantastic agent, Clare Wallace, and brilliant editors, Rebecca Hill and Becky Walker, deftly steered me along the right path and the story I wanted to tell began to emerge. Huge thanks to you all for believing in me and for your support – this book wouldn't exist without you!

Thank you to the Usborne marketing and publicity team and Fritha Lindqvist for promoting and publicizing this book so brilliantly. The cover art and illustrations are joyful and it was wonderful to see my home town of Bury St Edmunds being brought to life – thank you Kath Millichope, Sarah Cronin and Saara Katariina Söderlund for your incredible work.

I'm very grateful to the people at The Athenaeum (the Subscription Rooms) in Bury St Edmunds for giving me a guided tour of its Victorian observatory, and to the current occupiers of Cupola House, Sakura Japanese Restaurant, who kindly gave me access to the magnificent rooftop cupola which inspired the story.

Thank you to each and every writer, author, book blogger and promoter, teacher, librarian, journalist and bookseller who have championed my books. You are a lovely, supportive bunch and this writing lark wouldn't be half as fun without your friendship. Thanks also to the wonderful Usborne Books at Home team who have helped promote and sell my books – you're all marvellous!

Finally, a massive thanks to my family and friends, especially my endlessly supportive husband Jeremy for picking up my typos and terrible grammar. Mum and Dad, this book is dedicated to you. I very naughtily ripped up the books on your shelves when I was small, but you still managed to grow in me a love of reading and writing for which I will be forever grateful.